AF469834

SPECIAL MESSAGE TO READERS

This book is published under the auspices of

THE ULVERSCROFT FOUNDATION

(registered charity No. 264873 UK)

Established in 1972 to provide funds for research, diagnosis and treatment of eye diseases. Examples of contributions made are: —

A Children's Assessment Unit at Moorfield's Hospital, London.

•

Twin operating theatres at the Western Ophthalmic Hospital, London.

•

A Chair of Ophthalmology at the Royal Australian College of Ophthalmologists.

•

The Ulverscroft Children's Eye Unit at the Great Ormond Street Hospital For Sick Children, London.

You can help further the work of the Foundation by making a donation or leaving a legacy. Every contribution, no matter how small, is received with gratitude. Please write for details to:

THE ULVERSCROFT FOUNDATION,
The Green, Bradgate Road, Anstey,
Leicester LE7 7FU, England.
Telephone: (0116) 236 4325

In Australia write to:
THE ULVERSCROFT FOUNDATION,
c/o The Royal Australian and New Zealand
College of Ophthalmologists,
94-98 Chalmers Street, Surry Hills,
N.S.W. 2010, Australia

ANGEL HARVEST

Jennifer Dunbar's dream of becoming a successful lady jockey seems to be over when she has to quit to look after Ellie, her three-year-old niece. Ellie's mother, Rosamund, was killed during a thunderstorm. Mystery surrounds her death — and the identity of Ellie's father. Jennifer is determined to find him. But her search impacts upon other people, threatening to destroy not only their lives, but also her own. Then Jennifer discovers — too late — some secrets should remain secret . . .

Books by Glenis Wilson in the Linford Romance Library:

WEB OF EVASION
LOVE IN LAGANAS
THE HONEY TREE

GLENIS WILSON

ANGEL HARVEST

Complete and Unabridged

LINFORD
Leicester

First published in Great Britain in 2010

First Linford Edition
published 2010

British Library CIP Data

Wilson, Glenis.
Angel harvest. - - (Linford romance library)
1. Mothers- -Death- -Fiction.
2. Aunts- -Fiction. 3. Love stories.
4. Large type books.
I. Title II. Series
823.9'14–dc22

ISBN 978–1–44480–151–4

Published by
F. A. Thorpe (Publishing)
Anstey, Leicestershire

Set by Words & Graphics Ltd.
Anstey, Leicestershire
Printed and bound in Great Britain by
T. J. International Ltd., Padstow, Cornwall

This book is printed on acid-free paper

PROLOGUE

The white feather floated gently to earth.

Jennifer watched through blurred tear-filled eyes as it spiralled down, mesmerisingly slowly, to land soft and silent as a snowflake.

The grave-digger had wasted no time after the interment in back-filling the grave. The earth was mounded with a topping of turf. All the floral tributes were placed reverently on the grass, individual expressions of love for the young girl who lay beneath. She would remain anonymous until the ground had settled sufficiently to allow the erection of a headstone bearing her name: Rosamund.

The feather now rested on a heart-shaped wreath of roses — her own wreath. The contrast between the pure white and the crimson petals cupping it was stark — and so very beautiful.

Tears overflowed and slid down her cheeks. She blinked away any remaining teardrops, they were merely self-sympathy, not needed and inappropriate now.

Looking up into the richly blue summer sky, Jennifer was not surprised to see it was a blank canvas, completely empty. No clouds, no aeroplanes, no wind to have borne the feather and most significantly, no birds passing overhead.

Which meant only one thing . . .

1

'Hello, my angel!' Jennifer dropped her suitcase on the garden path and held wide both arms to engulf the little girl racing to meet her. The child's face was lit up with inner, joyful delight.

'Auntie Jen, Auntie Jen . . . ' She waved chubby dimpled arms wildly in excitement and the teddy bear clutched in her right hand was tossed and banged from side to side.

Jennifer's throat constricted as it always did at the sight of her three year old niece. Ellie was the living image of Rosamund, her mother. The likeness was bittersweet and never failed to move Jennifer, reminding her each time she would never again see her sister, never talk, share a confidence or a joke and a giggle. She fought back the distress. Children were so sensitive. It would be unforgiveable to project her emotions onto the little girl who was hurtling towards her.

'Steady, darling, steady,' she called the warning too late.

In her haste, Ellie tripped and tumbled into Jennifer's arms, laughing up into her face with glee. 'Kiss, kiss, Auntie Jen.'

Jennifer's arms tightened as she hugged the child fiercely, burying her face in the sweet-smelling cascade of golden curls. How very precious Ellie was now, the only living link with Rosamund.

And how very aware must her mother and father be that Ellie was the only grandchild they would ever have.

She gently set the child away from her. 'For you, darling, a rainbow of kisses.' She placed a kiss in the middle of the child's forehead.

Closing her eyes, Ellie said solemnly, 'Red.'

Jennifer kissed her left temple.

'Orange.'

The next kiss was in the middle of Ellie's cheek.

'Yellow,' she crowed, wriggling excitedly, pleased with herself for remembering the first three colours.

Green was planted on her chin, blue on her right cheek, indigo on the right temple and violet on her forehead.

'There, a whole rainbow of love just for you.'

The child sighed deeply with satisfaction. Then, opening one eye she looked up sideways, 'D'you know, Auntie Jen, you're the only one who *ever* kisses me a rainbow.'

'Am I?' Jennifer laughed giving her a last hug. 'Come on, take me to see Grandma. I bet she's made a pot of tea.'

She allowed herself to be tugged up the garden path to the back door leading into the kitchen. The cottage, surrounded by countryside in South Nottinghamshire, was old and very mellow. Built by her great-grandfather more than a hundred years ago, it was constructed from the locally-made red bricks. Regrettably, they were of a somewhat crumbly nature, as witness the odd brick that had lost its facing. Nevertheless, the rambling two-storey cottage was solidly built with a traditional and original slate roof.

The gardens were to the rear, a vegetable plot complete with apple and plum trees, lawns and flowerbeds running to over thirty metres. Beyond that the land extended to the rear and side in paddocks and the gallops.

To the side of the cottage was a large yard around the perimeter of which was an 'L' shaped run of stables.

This was home. Twenty-seven years ago she had been born here.

Looking round in the kitchen at the so-familiar old Aga, the Sheila rails above for drying and airing clothes, the big pine table with four chairs cuddling close, she could have been Ellie's age all over again. Nothing seemed changed, even the smell of ginger cake baking inside the cream cast-iron stove transported her back and gave a sense of peace and safety. Except that it hadn't proved safe for Rosamund and nothing could ever be the same again.

Over in the corner, a large golden retriever heaved himself up from a basket and wagged his way across the red quarries to press against her legs.

'He's pleased to see you.' Ellie patted the big dog with a small star-fish hand.

'I know he is. Dogs are so constant.' Jennifer rubbed his silky, buttermilk ears. 'Good boy, Sandy.'

'What's constant?'

'Always the same, reliable.' She smiled at the big dog. 'You know where you are with dogs. They never stop loving you.'

'I'm constant, too.' Ellie's bottom lip pushed out.

'Of *course* you are, sweetheart.'

The door to the living room opened and Mrs Dunbar came through. She was immediately pounced upon by Ellie.

'Grandma, Auntie Jen's come,' she jigged up and down. 'And I'm constant, like Sandy.'

'Aren't you just.' Mrs Dunbar's eyes met Jennifer's. 'I'm so glad you're here, me duck.'

Jennifer noted the lines of tiredness around her mother's eyes and felt smitten by guilt. She'd sat on that uncomfortable fence for several weeks feeling she should return, not wanting to. Until her father's brief and succinct telephone call a few days ago. 'Your mother can't cope, Jennifer. We need you.' Whether she felt ready to go back was immaterial. She had to return.

'It's lovely to see you, Mum.' They embraced warmly.

'How long can you stay?' It was said lightly but Jennifer knew how important her answer was.

'Let's mash some tea and we can talk.'

Her mother nodded. 'And we'll have some fresh cakes. They're ready.' She busied herself at the Aga whilst Jennifer poured out a jug of milk and set it on the waiting tea-tray.

'Am I in my old bedroom?'

Mrs Dunbar swung round. 'And where else would you be? It's your room.'

Jennifer experienced a sinking feeling, one of going down slowly, inexorably, beneath the waves. I'm being sucked back in, she thought, and had to fight back the feeling of suffocation. She gritted her teeth. 'I'll take my case up, before anyone falls over it. Be down straight away.'

'You've just brought the one case, have you?' Her mother didn't need to add anything more. The words hung in the air between them: if there's only one, you won't be staying long.

'It's alright, Mum,' Jennifer managed a smile, 'there's some more of my stuff outside in the Mini.'

Accompanied by a dancing Ellie, Jennifer climbed the narrow, twisting staircase and walked along the landing to the familiar room that had been, up to now, her sanctuary since she'd been born.

* * *

Mrs Dunbar was already pouring out tea when Jennifer entered the living room. Despite the warmth of late July, a small fire burned in the wide grate, an unshakeable family tradition, seeming to symbolise the very spirit of Swallow House and stables. The fire would progressively get larger as the weather worsened into autumn and by winter, would be the roaring, searing hot heart of the house drawing in and cocooning family and visitors alike.

As a child Jennifer had always thought nothing bad could ever happen to her family and their beloved home whilst ever the fire was alight. Now, with an adult's perception of life, she could see how illusory that belief had been.

Her mother held out some tea. 'I dare say you could really do with a nice strong cuppa after driving all that way.'

'Hmmm . . . ' Jennifer took the cup, 'I suppose Lambourn is a fair way.' She stirred the tea, allowing the mundane movement to claim her attention, not trusting herself to meet her mother's perceptive gaze. Lambourn had been a deliberate choice as a place to live and work after bolting. Near enough should she need to get back to Swallow Racing Stables yet far enough from the possibility of meeting with Hal. Hal Taylor. That name had been banned from her thoughts for almost a year. Now, forced back into them, his name had the power to set her hands shaking making the cup rattle against the saucer. Hastily, she put it down on the coffee table.

Mrs Dunbar offered round a delicious plateful of fresh-baked goodies. 'Try a ginger cake.' Jennifer gratefully took one.

Ellie beamed up at her, brown sticky crumbs clinging to her lips, 'Nice!'

'They certainly are. Grandma's a good cook, isn't she?' The child nodded vigorously.

The back door banged and seconds

later Peter Dunbar came in. A small wiry man dressed in scruffy jodhpurs, his insignificant appearance was at odds with the reality of his standing as a well-respected racehorse trainer.

'Dad!' Jennifer jumped up and rushed into his welcoming arms.

'Hello, lass, how're y'doing?'

Her face pressed against the rough fibre of his working shirt, nose filled with the sweet smell of horses, eyes filled with tears, Jennifer could only nod. He squeezed her shoulders understandingly. 'Great to have you home.'

'Auntie Jen's come back hasn't she, Granddad?'

'That's right, little 'un.'

At his words, Jennifer's tears overflowed, soaking into his shirt. This was proving so much more difficult than she'd anticipated. Her father's pet name for Rosamund had always been, 'little 'un.' Now it seemed he'd transferred the endearment to Ellie.

Rosamund's death three months before had hit all of them hard but her father had seemed to handle the grief. Suddenly, she wasn't so sure.

Choking back the tears, she pushed herself away within the circle of his arms. 'Time I was back, Dad, don't you think?'

'Aye, lass, high time. You can't keep running away from life. It's impossible anyroad, life's inside you. It goes everywhere with you.' He dropped a rare kiss on her forehead. 'If you don't eat yon ginger cake it's going to disappear.' He nodded towards Sandy who, drawn by the tantalising smell, was sitting beside her chair, eyes fixed on the cake and drooling madly.

'Oh no you don't, these are far too good.' Jennifer patted his head, but as he looked up with heart-melting pleading in his dark eyes, added, 'I'll save you a bit.'

Peter shook his head in mock despair. 'And I thought you were a tough lady jockey.'

'I am.'

'Talking about work,' Kathleen Dunbar

said, passing Peter a mug of tea, 'how does your Governor feel about you taking time off?'

'Not happy.' Jennifer bit into the cake.

'Shouldn't think he is, I know I wouldn't be.'

'But you rang me, Dad.' Jennifer murmured quietly. 'I've got to admit I felt bad letting Jackson down. We'd got a lot of runners out in the next couple of weeks.'

'Aye, I know. It's a matter of priorities . . . '

Kathleen frowned. 'What are you two talking about?'

'Nothing that concerns you, me duck.' Peter drained his mug. 'I'll get back down stables.' He raised an eyebrow at Jennifer. 'Coming?'

'Can you stop me?'

'Have I ever been able to? Strong-willed, that's what you are.'

'And who do I get that strong will from, eh?'

'Get away with you both,' Kathleen laughed.

'Can I come?' Ellie jumped up licking sticky fingers enthusiastically.

Peter ruffled her curls, ''Course you can.'

* * *

The stables ran down two sides of the yard. The shorter arm incorporated both tack and feed-room. At this time in the afternoon all was quiet, far removed from the bustling activity of early in the day.

At the sound of their footsteps on the concrete, two or three heads appeared over the open half-doors. The sight, as always, gave Jennifer an immediate lift of spirits.

All her life had been spent around horses and she couldn't imagine an existence without them because that's all it would be, an existence. She needed horses like other people needed food. Since her split with Hal Taylor it had been the horses that had carried her through so far and especially following Rosamund's sudden death.

Drawing in a deep breath she savoured the sweet smell of warm horse and hay and sighed with satisfaction.

A dark bay head swung over one of the stable doors. Blowing out wide velvet covered nostrils, the big animal gave a loud, reverberating whicker of recognition.

A wide grin spread over Jennifer's face. 'Hello, you.' She walked up to the stable door. 'Did you think I'd stay away from you, Dixie?' The horse blew gustily into her hair and she stroked his nose. 'Who's a lovely fella, then?'

Peter stood hands on hips watching them. 'I should have put Dixie on the phone to you weeks ago. Reckon it's him you've come back for.'

'Quite right.' Jennifer refused to rise to his baiting.

'Us too?' Ellie's little face was puckered with concern.

Not realising the little girl had been taking it all in, Jennifer swung the tot up into her arms and held her level with the horse's head.

'Give him a stroke, show him you love him — just like I love you and Grandma and Granddad.' Ellie's rigid body relaxed and she pressed her face against the horse's wide cheek. Dixie stood unmoving, eyes closed, as the child murmured endearments.

Peter came up behind Jennifer and put an arm round her shoulders.

'How long are you staying, me duck? 'Cos I do need to know. For both Kathleen's sake and little 'un's.'

Even without urgency in his voice, Jennifer knew the situation must be causing him great concern. His life was the stables and he was very much an outdoorsman. She knew even with his deep level of love for her mother, the brunt of looking after Ellie fell on Kathleen. Not a light task when you were approaching sixty. Although Ellie's obvious affinity with her grandparents was a blessing, her practical upbringing could be causing major problems.

She gently smoothed a tress of Ellie's

golden hair away from the questing whiffling lips of the big horse. There was no question of Dixie hurting the tot, he seemed ecstatic to be the receiver of such unconditional love being poured out to him.

'Please don't worry, Dad,' she whispered, 'I know where I'm supposed to be — right here.'

2

'A disturbed child? Whatever do you mean, Jennifer?' Kathleen frowned, 'I don't understand.'

Ellie had eventually been put to bed and the two women were enjoying a cosy after-dinner coffee all by themselves. Peter had taken himself off to the pub for a well-earned pint, something he had not been able to indulge in since Rosamund's death. He had taken his role as support to Kathleen very seriously, knowing that his help during the tough working day was minimal and the evening was the only time he had to do his bit.

Despite Kathleen's urgings that once in bed, the child was no trouble, he'd stubbornly refused.

'I know she's no trouble, Kath, but she can be . . . she is . . . demanding. Our two girls were a piece of cake to look after but now . . . ' He spread his hands.

Kathleen had looked down unable to meet his eyes or to refute his words. Trouble certainly wasn't the right word, Ellie was a delight, but she couldn't deny that the child needed a lot of attention and looking after.

However, now Jennifer was home, Peter was enjoying his first taste of freedom and real ale in three months.

'Come on, love, you can't leave it at that.' Kathleen topped up her coffee.

'I'm just trying to find the right way of putting it. It's a difficult subject.'

'I expect it is. Do you mean she should have specialist attention?'

'I didn't say anything about that.'

'Come on Jennifer love, credit me with a bit of intuition. I think Ellie's coping very well. And we both know she's pretty special.'

Jennifer nodded. 'Oh, believe me, Mum, she is. As our dear Rosamund's little girl, she's very precious to all of us. But her make-up is highly sensitive and I think we need to be aware how vulnerable she is. She's such a loving little soul. Have you noticed how large and intense her eyes are? They're truly amazing. When she looks into your eyes she seems to be able to see right through to your soul.'

Kathleen nodded, 'Oh yes, from the moment Ellie was born, she looked straight at Rosamund for several minutes and then turned her eyes on me. Her gaze was so intent.' She shook her head in wonderment as she remembered. 'I know babies can't focus immediately. And yet this little one really seemed to be trying to focus on our faces.' Kathleen leaned forward excitedly now. 'And she never blinked, Jennifer, she just held our eyes. I remember her gaze felt, well, hypnotic.'

The two women sat silently thinking about the little girl upstairs and, inevitably, about Rosamund.

'Mum,' Jennifer reached for the poker and stirred the fire before adding a log, 'did you ever find out who Ellie's father was?'

'I wish.' Her mother sighed. 'All we know is the man must be local, I mean, Rosamund was only sixteen when she became pregnant, still at school.'

'I know . . . what a shock it must have been for her. Just about to start out on life herself and to find she was going to give life to another human being . . . '

'It broke her up to begin with but then . . . strange now I come to think about it, at some point in her pregnancy she seemed to draw comfort from the baby itself.

'She'd go very dreamy and withdrawn, put both hands around her bump and sit in silence for long periods. Didn't answer if your dad or I spoke to her. To be honest, I don't think she even heard us. But it wasn't a depressed silence. She'd be smiling softly to herself and often she seemed to murmur secretly, just her lips moving, no actual words being spoken.'

‘Yes, I know what you mean,’ Jennifer nodded thoughtfully. ‘I think Rosamund would have been talking to the baby.’

‘Really?’

‘Hmmm . . . Didn’t you ever do that when you were expecting us?’

‘It’s possible, but do you know, Jennifer, I can’t remember.’

‘Whoever her father was, Ellie brought a lot of love with her.’

‘Oh she did! Rosamund found a great deal of happiness in her baby. They seemed cocooned together in their own world. She certainly appreciated every minute to the full. Strange really,’ Kathleen shook her head a little, ‘almost as if somehow she knew their time together was short.’

‘After Ellie was born, did it take her a long time to begin to talk? With being away a lot racing and certainly the whole of this last year, I wouldn’t know.’

Kathleen put down the empty coffee cup and lay back in the armchair, ‘I’m not sure. She was never a child who chattered a lot. She seemed to know what I wanted her to do, almost before I'd thought it myself. Or if I said I wondered what we were going to have for lunch say, she'd go toddling off to the fridge and try to open the door. She couldn't of course, but when the door was opened she'd put her hand in and bring out, perhaps, a tomato, offer it to me — and just look at me. She wouldn't speak — just look.'

'Obviously, she was trying to communicate just through her actions.'

Both women were silent, thinking about Kathleen's words.

From upstairs came a thin cry followed by a sob. Kathleen started up in her chair. 'She has nightmares.'

'Losing your mum at three years old would guarantee nightmares, I should think.' Jennifer lightly pushed her mother's shoulder. 'My turn, I'm here to help.'

Kathleen sank back gratefully. 'I can't pretend I'm not very relieved. I love her so much and since losing Rosamund, well, she's such a comfort, but I'm not twenty anymore.'

Another shrill wail hastened Jennifer through the staircase door and upstairs. She snapped on the bedroom light. Ellie was sitting up in bed, fists pressed to her eyes, her whole body shaking.

'Everything's OK, darling. Auntie Jen's here.' She sat down on the bed and swung her legs up onto the duvet. Gathering the distressed child into her arms she cuddled her close.

Ellie struggled, 'Grandma, want Grandma.' She strung out the words between sobs.

'I know, darling,' Jennifer pressed her closer stroking the child's hair. 'You're safe and I love you, everything's alright. It was a silly dream. Grandma's downstairs sitting by the fire. She's allowed me to come upstairs to see you. Isn't that kind of her?' The sobs slowed and the child nodded. Jennifer continued to hold her close, softly singing a soothing lullaby as she stroked Ellie's hair. Seeking reassurance, the child buried her face against her and Jennifer felt overwhelmed with protective love. The child needed a mother and whilst she could never take Rosamund's place, she could do her very best to act as proxy.

A few moments later Ellie twisted round and turned tear-flooded eyes up at her. 'Tired, Auntie Jen.' Jennifer smiled and nodded. Ellie wriggled down lower in the bed and laid her head in Jennifer's lap. 'Nice, nice . . . ' she murmured sleepily.

Within minutes the tot had drifted off into a peaceful sleep. Jennifer eased herself out of the encircling, trusting arms and slid from the bed. Pulling the duvet up over Ellie's shoulders, she put the light out and went back down the twisty staircase.

'All OK?'

'Gone off to sleep more or less straight away.'

'You certainly seem to have the soothing touch.'

Jennifer smiled. 'Not really, Ellie was tired out.'

Kathleen stood up and put her arms round her daughter. 'You have a way with her that we older ones don't have. And I'm so very glad you've decided to come back. It's going to be a boon, you returning home. Your dad and me couldn't cope with bringing up Ellie without you. Yes, I know I'm putting pressure on you but it's the truth. And if Ellie is a bit disturbed, and it seems she may well be, it's doubly important for us that you're here.'

Jennifer hugged her back. 'It's not a pressure, or something I want to run away from, not now I've come back and seen how you've been struggling. What more satisfying job can you do than help bring up a sensitive child like Ellie? She's gorgeous.'

'But,' Kathleen hesitated, 'what about . . . Hal?'

'What about him?'

'Jennifer love, you're bound to bump into him. I mean, he only lives a couple of miles down the lane.'

'So?'

Kathleen looked troubled. 'We need you here, love, but we don't want to cause you pain.'

'Look, Mum, both myself and Hal were born here. We're equally entitled to live on this particular patch.

'I shall try to avoid meeting him if it's humanly possible but if I do, well, maybe he won't want to meet me, either. OK, when we split, I bolted. We needed space apart and, practically speaking, it would have been impossible for Hal to up and go. He's got to run the family farm.'

'I know.'

'But, circumstances have changed now Rosamund's gone; naturally, you've turned to me, and so I've come back. Not to rake over the embers, but because for one thing, Ellie needs me and for another, it's my home.'

'Bless you. It will make the world of difference to dear Ellie. She misses her mum.'

'As far as I'm concerned, ideally, a child needs two parents; certainly one at least, But right now, she hasn't either. Now I'm back, I fully intend to find out who her father is.'

'You said you don't want to rake over old embers, Jennifer. It could cause a lot of trouble if you do find out.'

'I'll be very discreet, don't fret. And I wasn't talking about Rosamund's embers, but my own.'

Kathleen nodded. 'I know, but are those still . . . glowing?'

Jennifer poured out a fresh coffee and sweetened it with a spoonful of honey. 'Ask me again, when I've met him.'

* * *

Kathleen was first up in the morning, she'd always been an early riser. Lifting the cover on the Aga she pushed the kettle onto the heat. A few minutes later she handed a mug of sweet black coffee to Peter as he came into the kitchen yawning hugely.

'Not used to it, that's your problem,' she joked.

'Go on with you, woman. I can hold my beer as well as the next man.' He sank down heavily into a kitchen chair. 'Jennifer up yet?'

'No, but I did hear her get up in the night with Ellie.'

'She says her place is here, told me yesterday, down in the stables.'

'Well last night while you were down at the Black Swan, I was saying we needed help with Ellie and she said it wasn't a problem.'

'What will be a problem is Jackson.' He gulped coffee. 'I don't know how he's going to react. But I do know she should still be race riding. She's worked hard to get to this point. I don't want her throwing away her chances because of us.' He scraped back his chair. 'Be in later for breakfast, love.' He gave her a quick kiss and took himself off to the stables.

* * *

'Eat a little bit more of the moon, Ellie,' Jennifer urged. She'd cut small triangles from a slice of wholemeal and toasted the resulting star-shaped piece of bread. Curved around it on the little plate, she'd formed scrambled egg into a sickle moon. Ellie, as she'd expected, was a very picky eater.

'Well, bless me,' Kathleen leaned back against the sink unit and shook her head. 'I'd never have thought of trying that. I usually boil an egg in an egg cup and believe me, it's such a battle to get her to eat even a little bit of it.'

'First rule of winning, know the strengths and weaknesses of the competition.'

'Juice, juice,' Ellie demanded. Kathleen poured her a refill.

'So, what's the agenda today? We'd better sort out some sort of division of duties. Obviously, you're far better at getting food down.'

'Would you mind, Mum, if I did breakfast and then disappeared down the stables? I know I've missed first lot but I could ride out on second.'

'Just like your father, can't keep away from the horses.'

'Can't risk losing my race fitness. I was thinking it all through last night — '

'You mean, the early hours,' Kathleen smiled in commiseration. 'Oh yes, I know you got up with her.'

'Sorry, did I wake you?'

'No, love, I must be conditioned to waking around that time. I'm afraid Ellie does suffer disturbed sleep.'

'Hmmm . . . there are one or two things I can try,' Jennifer mused.

'You were saying, about thinking things through.'

'Oh, oh yes. Well, I do need to earn a living of course, and I was thinking if I still keep myself fit and free for available rides that might work quite well.'

'What about Jackson?'

'Ah, now that's the big one. I suppose he's not going to need to know for at least a week because I'm on two weeks leave at the moment.'

'I see.'

'But the second week will probably have to be used in lieu of notice.'

'No, Jennifer, definitely, no. He deserves a working notice.'

'I know he does, but I can't be in two places at once.'

'We can easily manage for a week if we know you're coming back.'

'Yes, I suppose. And I'd certainly feel better if I could work my notice.'

'Are you going to give him a ring, let him know the situation?'

Jennifer bent over to lift Ellie down from her chair, grateful for the opportunity to avoid her mother's eyes. It had been one thing to acknowledge that her duty undoubtedly was here at home but she knew there was also her own needs to be considered. Apart from the chance she could easily bump into Hal — what effect that might have on her was too scary to consider — she didn't relish throwing away her racing career. It had taken too long to build up and at considerable personal and emotional cost.

Putting that all-important race first last year had certainly put her on the map as regards being considered a talented professional lady jockey but its down side had spelt death to her relationship with Hal. Her decision on the course of her life right now was vitally important and involved the not insignificant matter of her own sense of self-worth and self-respect. To sacrifice herself entirely was not the answer to the present problem. She had put her career in race riding first before Hal and if she gave it up now she would have lost both.

She also knew she was fence-sitting again, this time on the matter of informing Jackson of a final decision regarding her job at his stables in Lambourn.

'I'll talk it over with Dad tonight. See what he says. His view won't be biased. Perhaps mine is.'

'Jennifer, love, if you don't do what

you personally want to, it's not going to work. You'll end up feeling resentful and maybe cheated out of your life. Because that's what we're talking here — your life.'

Jennifer went up and put her arms round her mother giving both of them a comforting hug. 'Believe me, I understand exactly what you're saying. It's the same thing I'm telling myself. That's why it's such a difficult decision to make.'

'And you can tell me to shut up but I think if all your embers haven't finally gone out, you should consider seeing Hal — before you make that decision.'

Jennifer backed off, holding both palms in the air. 'I'm going off to the stables. The good thing about horses is they don't try giving you advice.'

Kathleen laughed. 'Have a good ride. See you back for lunch.'

3

Jennifer ran down the twisty staircase. After a strenuous morning's work, a quick five minute shower had taken away the smell of stables and refreshed her. The temperature outside was high and rising, tiring both humans and horses.

Kathleen was putting out plates of hot wholemeal toast with spaghetti in tomato sauce and in the centre of the table was a dish piled high with freshly grated mature cheddar cheese. 'Get on alright, love?' She placed a generous helping in front of Jennifer.

'Hmm, lovely to ride my old familiars again. I was riding work on Dixie and I'd say he'll do a walk-over in a six furlong. He's come on so much since I last rode him.'

Ellie, following her granddad's lead, reached across for a serving spoonful of cheese and scattered it liberally on top of her spaghetti. 'I like this,' she informed Jennifer solemnly, nodding her head, ' 's nice.'

'Are you saving some for me?'

'Yes, and some for Grandma.'

'Oh good,' Kathleen sat down at the table and sighed.

'Everything OK this morning?' Peter asked.

Kathleen pursed her lips, 'I'm just a bit tired. I think it's the heat and Ellie's feeling it too.'

Jennifer met her dad's eyes and read the message in them. 'After lunch, I think I'll take Ellie out in the pushchair for a walk. I'll put the sunshade over to keep her nice and shaded.'

'That would be lovely, Jennifer. I think I'll take a doze with Peter whilst you're in charge.'

'Seconded.' Peter helped himself to more cheese. 'We've no runners today, so I'm certainly going to get a nap in. Won't get the chance tomorrow. We're at Leicester racecourse.'

'How many runners have we?' Jennifer ground some black pepper on top of her spaghetti.

'Two, Morning Cloud and Dixie. Marcus Knowles is riding Morning Cloud and Will Banbury's on Dixie.'

Jennifer held down a sudden sharp spurt of jealousy. She'd be getting a race ride soon enough but she was a competitive jockey and Dixie had always been her ace horse. 'What time will the horse-box be leaving?'

'Around ten. Leicester's not far and we're not in until the 3.30.'

Knowing how her daughter's mind worked, Kathleen said, 'I don't mind in the least if you want to go along, Jennifer.'

'Me go?' Ellie had been listening to the conversation, her gaze swivelling first to one then another, whilst eating her meal with gusto. Scooping up the last of her grated cheese, she added in all seriousness, 'It's in the blood.'

There was a moment's silence before they all burst out laughing.

'Where *did* she get that from?' Jennifer asked.

'From Peter, I suspect.'

'That's right, blame me.' He grinned.

'Yes,' Ellie nodded placing her cutlery neatly side by side on her empty plate. 'I was in the stable loving Popeye an' granddad said, it's in the blood.' She looked at them earnestly with her enormous expressive eyes, ' 'S true.' Popeye was a grey with wall-eyes who was in the last stable next to the tack room. He had a questionable temperament but with Ellie he was a softie.

'I'm sure it is, darling.' Kathleen gave the child a kiss and lifted her down from the table.

'Want to go and see Popeye now.' Ellie struggled from Kathleen's arms and rushed to the door.

'Not now, Ellie.'

'Yes, yes.' The child's voice rose. 'I want to go now.' Kathleen bit her lip and looked across at Peter.

'Not now, Ellie,' Jennifer said gently, 'Popeye's fast asleep. He's been a busy boy this morning, you know, galloping up and down.'

Ellie pouted and smacked the door with a flat hand, 'Want to.' Her eyes flooded with tears.

'Tell you what,' Jennifer went to the cloakroom and came back with the pushchair and Ellie's sun hat, 'you pop your hat on and we'll go out for a walk.'

'Can I take Loppy-lugs?'

'Her toy rabbit,' Peter whispered.

'Sure you can. We can't go without him, can we? He'll cry if we leave him behind.'

Ellie scampered off to retrieve the furry toy.

'Now you see why we want you here. Our patience level isn't as high as yours.'

Jennifer smiled at her dad. 'Don't forget, you've already been through all this once bringing us up.'

'True enough,' he sighed. 'And anytime I start to feel irritated or annoyed with the child, it's then I remember Rosamund's no longer here.'

Meeting Kathleen's eye, he shrugged. 'And, well, I feel . . . worse.' He walked to the window and stared out moodily.

'You two have a nice afternoon nap,' Jennifer said briskly, putting the plates in the sink and running hot water. 'Ellie will be absolutely fine when I get her outside in the fresh air.'

'Reckon you'd best not take her too far. Looks to me like we could have a storm brewing up, it's gone very hazy.'

'I'll take care.'

'Found him, look, look.' Ellie dashed into the kitchen waving a chocolate brown bunny with outrageously long ears. 'And I've put my hat on Auntie Jen.' She paraded round the kitchen.

'Right, hop in your pushchair, we'll get off straight away.'

* * *

Her father had been right, thought Jennifer as she settled into a rhythmic walk down the lane. The best of the day's bright sunshine had gone and the air felt hot and heavy. Over to the west the sky had a bruised look. However, it was lovely to be out walking in her home territory again. She'd enjoyed her rides earlier on the familiar gallops spreading away at the back of the stables. It all felt so right. She knew this decision was easy to make but nothing was ever simple; one decision inevitably led to other consequences. A picture of Hal's face came into her mind. Resolutely, she pushed it away. There were plenty of other problems associated with her return. But for now, they could all be filed. She was going to enjoy the freedom of being out with Ellie. She bent forward. 'Alright, angel?'

The child was singing softly to herself, hugging Loppy-lugs close. She lifted her face and gave a beatific smile. A wave of love swamped Jennifer. What did her own problems matter? Picking up the lilt of the song, she joined in and, contentedly singing in duet, they made their way down the dusty lane between the fields.

Coming to the end of a verse of the song, Jennifer realised she was singing by herself. Without slowing her steps, she angled forward to peek at Ellie. The little girl was fast asleep, eyelashes sweeping a curtain over her blue eyes, a soft pink glow on her cheeks.

Jennifer offered a prayer that the sleep would be sweet and free from the nightmares that plagued her. Deep restorative sleep was so important to a young child. Obviously, the warmth of the day had lulled Ellie off, no doubt combined with the movement of the pushchair, but Jennifer was particularly gratified that Ellie had clearly felt sufficiently secure and safe in her company to do so. She wouldn't turn for home yet, far better for Ellie to gain the benefit of an extended peaceful nap.

Coming to the narrow crossroads in the lane, she turned right from old habit and wandered on down the tree-lined shady green tunnel that glinted gold every now and again as the hazy sun found a way through the dense summer foliage.

Her thoughts freed now from responsibility ranged around her favourite topic — race riding. It was not something she could give up, for too long it had filled all her waking moments. Knowing her mother and father would not wish her to either filled her with a strength and determination to be able to fulfil both roles now demanded of her. With every new step forward her spirits lifted and she felt instinctively everything would work out fine.

Half an hour later she found herself facing a five-barred gate leading into a long winding track through a copse. Jennifer hesitated. She had been immersed in thoughts of riding at a top track like Windsor or Goodwood. Now feeling slightly disorientated, she looked about her and realised the sunshine had vanished altogether, the sky was a sullen dark blanket of grey and sulphur and the bruising to the west had galloped across the sky and was pressing up to the other side of the copse. There was an ominous stillness holding everything in limbo.

'Oh no!' Jennifer breathed deeply. The threatening storm wasn't simply approaching, it had all but arrived. And she was acutely aware they were a long way from home.

A tendril of hair blew across her face. Whereas a second ago it had seemed so still, now a slight breeze disturbed that stillness. Within moments the wind increased in strength, first teasing then tossing the branches of the trees in the copse in front of her. It came as a jolt to realise where the unfocussed wandering had led her.

Here at the edge of the wood, Rosamund's body had been discovered. And it would have been in similar circumstances. The unexpected storm which had blown up three months ago had brought down a massive branch from an elm tree. Rosamund, it was assumed, had been sheltering from the torrential rain when the lightning had struck the tree. She had stood no chance. The branch had hit her across the head. The doctor who had delivered the news of her injuries had said she would have known nothing about it. Death would have been instantaneous. It was the only aspect of comfort.

The three of them, Peter, Kathleen and Jennifer had been so utterly shocked that it hadn't been until much later that the question of what Rosamund was doing in the wood had been voiced.

Ellie had been left in Kathleen's care that afternoon, her mother expected back by dinnertime. Despite the weather, neither Peter nor Kathleen had been concerned until it had passed six o'clock and the dinner keeping warm in the Aga was forming a drying crust. Peter's agitated phone call had brought Jennifer up from Lambourn just before midnight.

Rosamund's body had been found the following morning.

The rush of graphically sharp images

in her mind left Jennifer shaking. What irony had brought her here today? But it wasn't Rosamund's death alone that was distressing her. She'd hacked over this back way in the days she'd been seeing Hal. His farmland boundary began here at the edge of the wood.

A sudden howling gust of wind had the trees bowing over and brought Jennifer back to the immediate moment. The danger from the oncoming storm was now imminent. She had to get herself and Ellie out of here to somewhere safe. But where? The wood itself was certainly not safe. She looked round frantically. Over the other side of the field beyond the wood was a big barn, its roof just visible above the slope of the ground.

Jennifer groaned inwardly. If only there were some other place of safety. The old barn was the last place she would have chosen to go. The memories of times past spent within the shelter of its walls were sweet to the extreme — or would have been had she and Hal still been together. As a single woman now, those memories were acid-sharp and tormenting.

A single fat drop of rain splashed down on the back of her wrist where she held the handle of the pushchair. She had no luxury of choice, action was required, and fast.

Pushing open the small hand-gate entrance at the side of the five-barred gate, she angled the pushchair through. Thankfully, it was sturdily built, having big wheels with pneumatic tyres that rode over all but the larger tussocks of grass as Jennifer circled the copse and headed down the slope. A low growl of thunder seemed to follow her running feet and a few seconds later fork lightning ripped across the now indigo coloured sky.

The raindrops were pattering down heavily and steadily increasing as, panting with exertion, she reached the barn and unlatched the stable-type door. The interior was dim and dusty but, thankfully, dry and would provide all the safety they needed from the earth-seeking lightning. She thrust the pushchair over the lip of the doorway.

Along the back wall the disc harrow was drawn up awaiting the next season's work and over in the farthest corner, covered in a veil of cobwebs and mouldering gently into obscurity, was a wooden milk cart. In its working life, probably seventy years ago, it had carried the milk churns down from the farm to the entrance gates to await collection by the milk lorry.

Jennifer eased the pushchair over to the corner where a small pile of hay bales were stacked alongside the bale cart. Miraculously, Ellie was still deeply and blissfully asleep. Jennifer secured the brake and perched herself on the wooden base of the bale cart that was covered in a loose scattering of hay. If she was in for a long wait whilst the storm passed over, she could at least make herself as comfortable as possible.

The rain was peppering the roof of the barn with an increased intensity now and Jennifer was relieved that they had made it just in time. She closed her eyes the better to savour their extremely lucky escape. The barn had an enclosed secure feel and she was very grateful they were dry and safe inside. Her last words to her parents replayed in her head, 'I'll take care.' She shivered. They had come very close to being caught out in the full force of the storm's fury.

The sound of a horse's hoof beats drumming across the field and rapidly approaching had her eyes opening in surprise. Seconds later, the barn door swung wide and a horse clattered in. The man riding it kicked his feet free of the stirrup irons and slid from the wet saddle. He pulled off a hard hat and dashed raindrops from his face before drawing the reins over the horse's head. Leading it over to a ring in the wall, he looped the reins through.

Only then did he turn and look about him.

Their eyes met — and locked.

'Jennifer!' he exclaimed.

‘Hello, Hal,’ she said, shakily.

A tremendous clap of thunder seemed to shake the barn, followed instantaneously by fork lightning that illuminated the sky.

And above the sound of the torrential rain beating hard upon the roof came a piercing scream of terror, rising in volume until it seemed to fill the entire barn.

4

The horse half-reared, snatched at its bridle and gave a loud neigh of fright.

'What in the world is that?' Hal's shocked eyes bore into hers.

But Jennifer dragged her gaze from his face, slid down from the wooden cart and dropped to her knees.

'Darling, it's alright.' She reached for Ellie and hugged her close. 'Auntie Jen's here, you're safe.' But the child would not be placated. She continued to scream, tears pouring down her reddened cheeks. Lifting her from the restraints of the pushchair, Jennifer sat on the dusty floor, took the child onto her lap and rocked back and forth hugging her tightly.

The horse continued to stamp and whinny, upset by the storm and the child's cries. Hal went to its side running a hand down the sweating neck and spoke soothingly to it.

'Don't cry, Ellie, you're safe.' Small hands grasped in agitation at Jennifer's T-shirt.

'Mummy, Mummy's hurt,' Ellie shrilled.

Hal left the horse and came over to hunker down beside them. 'What's she saying? Whose child is it, I wonder?'

'Hush, darling, hush,' Jennifer cradled the child to her breast. Turning her face to Hal she said, 'Don't you *know?*' Their faces were barely inches apart. She could even feel his breath on her cheek. Treacherous feelings began to well up inside her. 'But you must do.'

He shook his head, 'No, no I don't.'

'It's my sister's little girl. Ellie is Rosamund's daughter.'

Hal looked stricken. 'This is . . . Rosamund's baby?'

Jennifer nodded, suddenly choked with a surfeit of emotions. Quite unable to stop herself, she began to cry.

The feelings she had bottled up deep within, pretending she could get over losing Hal, so soon followed by losing her sister, surged to the surface and completely overwhelmed her. The raging grief was a physical pain ripping her apart. Through a mist of tears, she saw Hal reach out and felt his hand cover hers.

'Cry it out, Jenny,' he said gently. 'Let it go, you'll feel better.'

Oddly, Ellie's cries had ceased and she looked up into Jennifer's face with deep concern. 'Mummy's alright now, Auntie Jen.' She patted her face softly in a comforting gesture. Jennifer caught the small hand and held it to her lips.

'Bless you, my angel,' she wept.

'Like my nasty dream, gone now,' Ellie nodded, 'all gone.'

Hal was looking at the little girl in amazement. 'By, you've an old head on young shoulders.'

Ellie transferred her attention to him. 'Auntie Jen's crying, isn't she? She's upset.'

He bent down to her level. 'You and

me will have to comfort her, don't you think?'

'Yes, I'm going to give her a kiss.' And she pressed her face against Jennifer's wet cheeks and planted a sloppy kiss. Drawing back she beamed, 'Better now.' Then she swung round to Hal. 'You kiss Auntie Jen better, too.'

'No, no,' Jennifer struggled to gain control. 'You've kissed me better now.'

'I could give you a kiss, too, just to make sure,' Hal suggested.

'Just to make sure,' Ellie repeated, nodding.

And before Jennifer could protest, he'd leaned forward, caught her face between his palms and brushed his lips across hers. Taking a deep breath he released her. Jennifer felt a shiver run the length of her body leaving her weak-kneed. She was very grateful that she was sitting down. There was a long crashing roll of thunder above their heads.

Hal glanced ruefully upwards. 'Afraid it's still with us.' Then he hesitated and looked directly at Jennifer. 'Wouldn't you agree?' A warm depth glowed within his eyes that irresistibly drew her down, threatening to drown her.

'Possibly,' she said, adding firmly, 'but I'm quite sure it's on its way out.'

He drew back a little and the warmth died. 'You could be right,' he said stiffly. 'But in the meantime, we're all of us stuck here in the barn.'

'How come you're here?'

'I could ask you the same.'

'We were out for a walk and got caught out with the storm. The barn was the only place to shelter.'

'You've walked a good way, why this direction?'

Colour flooded Jennifer's cheeks. She shrugged. 'I've no idea.'

'I have,' he said in a low voice. 'It's called force of habit. Or it could be your unconscious led you back.'

'Don't flatter yourself, Hal. The poor child suffers nightmares and she'd gone off to sleep. I was trying to give her chance to top up with a peaceful nap.'

His face softened with compassion. 'I guess it's to be expected. I mean, losing your mother at that age.' He shook his head. 'A tragedy.'

'That's why I've come home, to help to look after Ellie. A child needs parents and she's as good as an orphan because we don't know who her father is.' She covertly watched his face for any reaction. There was a slim chance he might have heard some rumour whilst she'd been away in Lambourn. But his expression didn't alter.

'Rosamund kept his name a secret, then?'

'Hmm, but Mum and Dad reckon it must have been a local man. Well, local at that time. It's four years ago now.'

'I shouldn't think there's much chance of finding out now.'

'Left to me, I'd have a DNA test done on the entire male population in this area. That's how strongly I feel about it. Why should he do what he liked with Rosamund and then ignore Ellie. It's not right!'

'If you were a horse, you'd be stamping a hoof right now.'

'I certainly feel like stamping my foot but it wouldn't set a very good example to Ellie.'

They both looked at the child but she was taking no notice of either of them. Still cradled on Jennifer's lap, she'd fallen back to sleep.

'Oh, to be a child again with no responsibilities — and someone to look after you, love you.'

It wasn't so much Hal's words that touched Jennifer as the look in his eyes. They held a sad yearning he could not disguise.

'How is your mother?'

Mary Taylor had been ten years older than Daniel, Hal's father, when they had married. She had given birth to three children: Hal, the oldest, Anthony and the youngest, Anya, the only girl. The marriage had been an exceptionally happy one, the family close knit, until about four years ago when Daniel had died suddenly from cancer of the liver.

At that point, Mary had given up, sunk in a depressive state from which she had never recovered. The bulk of her care had fallen upon Anya, who still lived at home and wasn't married. Anthony, never interested in farming, had married and gone to work for his father-in-law's computer company in London. Hal was left to run the farm.

'Some days she's better than others,' he replied. And then added, 'But I don't think she'll ever get better, Jenny.'

'I do hope she will, Hal. I'm so very sorry for all of you. Your dad was the love of her life . . . '

They looked at each other and in the silence that stretched between them, Jennifer's words seemed to echo and re-echo.

'Despite what happened to Dad, they were lucky. Twenty-five years of wedded bliss and they were more in love then than when they met. Most people can only dream of that sort of love.'

'I think the storm's over, the rain's

stopped.' Jennifer dare not trust herself to continue to look at him.

Hal got to his feet. 'You could be right. But everywhere will be sopping wet. I suggest you two girls stay here whilst I ride back to the farm and swap horsepower for an engine and four wheels. Then I can run you both home.'

'You don't need to, Hal. I can walk back.'

'I wouldn't hear of it. The old lane is quite likely to be flooded. It isn't fit for a pushchair.'

She nodded. 'I guess you're right.'

'Sure I am.'

He smiled. 'Let the little one sleep until I get back, she looks very peaceful cuddled up on your lap.'

'Dad called her that, 'little 'un,' Jennifer said in a low voice.'

'Isn't that what he used to call your sister, Rosamund?'

She bit on her lip and nodded. 'It broke me up when I got back and heard him say it.'

'And now I've said it, too. It was thoughtless of me. I'm really sorry. I should have been more sensitive.' The warmth was back in his eyes. 'I still care for you, Jenny.'

'Please don't, Hal. We can't go back and my life's complicated enough.'

'And that's what I'd be, is it, a 'complication'?'

'No, I didn't mean . . . oh, I don't know what I mean. Except I can't handle any more emotional situations right now.'

'Why should it be an additional burden? You might find I could help you shoulder some of the difficulties you're facing.'

'You and I would have to face the same problem we faced once before. It hasn't gone away even though I've come back home. You're wedded to the farm, you always will be.'

He spread his hands helplessly. 'I have no choice, it's my life. Without the farm, what would happen to Mother and Anya?'

'And I respect your commitment, Hal.'

'Well, then . . . '

'No, No, Hal, we'd only end up hurting each other again.'

His shoulders slumped. 'That is the very last thing I want to do.' He went over to the horse, unhooked the reins and led the animal out.

Seated on the floor Jennifer watched him go. She gave him a few minutes then cautiously eased herself onto her knees and, hugging Ellie closer, levered herself up. Gently settling the child in the pushchair, she released the brake and pushed it across the barn and out of the doorway.

The sky was now a clear brilliant blue. Underfoot, the grass was soaking wet and to cross the field on foot would certainly have wrecked her flimsy sandals. It would have been far safer not to see Hal again but, she acknowledged, right now she was grateful for his help in getting them home safe and dry. It would undoubtedly have proved extremely unpleasant walking the couple of miles along the flooded lanes.

She could hear the sound of the Land Rover's engine as it approached, labouring somewhat as it traversed the steep slope up to the barn. And then he was there, smiling through the windscreen as he swung the wheel and backed the vehicle right up to where she stood waiting.

'Your taxi, m'Lady.' He scooped Ellie from the pushchair. 'In you get, Jenny.'

When she was sitting in the passenger seat, he placed the child onto her knee and reaching around them both, secured the seat belt. Taking the pushchair round to the rear door he swung it aboard and came back to slide into the driver's seat.

'OK?' he raised an eyebrow. She nodded, acutely aware of his closeness, especially so when his arm brushed her own as he engaged first gear.

His attention now, however, was focussed on driving as the tyres skidded a little on the long wet grass. He left the engine in first gear and crawled up over the slope and turned onto the wide track through Keeper's Copse. The vehicle bounced on the uneven rutted surface and Jennifer held Ellie closer, cupping the child's head to avoid jerking her awake.

At the end of the copse, Hal jumped down to open the five-barred gate. If it hadn't been for nursing her, Jennifer would have been out of the vehicle and doing the duty of opening and closing the gate. It felt very strange to be waited on and looked after but at the same time it gave her a strange, comforting warm feeling inside to feel she could leave the responsibility to him. It was a long time since she'd been able to lean on anyone. And hard on that thought came another one. If she could forget the past and enter a relationship again with Hal, she could experience this feeling of being cherished all the time.

Looking sideways at him as he drove

them carefully back through the accurately predicted flooded lanes, she knew the embers she'd assiduously damped down were still glowing.

Feeling her eyes on him Hal glanced quickly at her and smiled. Her heart stepped up its rhythm. 'It's a pity, but we'll be at Swallow House in a couple of minutes.'

'You like driving at twenty miles an hour, then?'

'With you beside me, yes.'

At his words a picture rose in her mind of the last time she had been in a car with him. But Ellie suddenly awoke with a thrashing of arms and squirming body, and the recollection vanished as her attention was immediately diverted to holding onto the child.

'Is she alright?' Hal asked turning the Land Rover in through the wide gates of the stable yard.

'Oh yes, she just wondered where she was for a minute. Didn't you, my sweet?' Jennifer dropped a kiss on the child's head.

'I'm with you, Auntie Jen.'

'That's right.'

'Who are you?' She pointed a finger at Hal. 'What's your name?'

'Hush, Ellie, it's rude to point at someone.'

'But I don't know your name,' the child persisted, frowning.

'Well, I know yours. It's Ellie Dunbar. And mine's Hal Taylor.' He thrust out a big hand. 'I'm very pleased to know you.'

Her frown disappeared replaced by a happy smile. 'I remember,' she said, putting her small one in his and pumping it up and down. 'You kissed Auntie Jen in the barn.'

Hal was still chuckling as he pushed the pushchair round to the kitchen door. Ellie ran in front of Jennifer calling loudly for her grandma.

Kathleen appeared in the open doorway. Her face was a picture when she saw Hal. She had always had a soft spot for the quiet farmer and could never understand why Jennifer had returned home one day in a distressed state minus her engagement ring and announced she was going away.

She'd been bewildered. What was so awful that Hal had done to provoke such an extreme reaction in her daughter? She couldn't image him doing anything hurtful. Hal had a placid, dependable temperament and she'd been overjoyed when Jennifer had chosen him for her future husband. To see him pushing her granddaughter's pushchair and following Jennifer through the kitchen door was so unexpected. Did this mean their engagement was back on? Her heart jumped with happiness. It would be so wonderful.

'Where would you like me to park Ellie's wheels?'

'It lives in the downstairs cloakroom, Hal, thanks.'

As he disappeared she turned to Jennifer with eyebrows raised and unspoken questions written on her face. But before either could speak, Peter came downstairs.

'Any tea going?'

Kathleen's face relaxed into a smile. 'Coming up. Shall I make tea for four?'

'Eh?'

'You'd better ask Hal,' Jennifer murmured.

'Tea?' Kathleen queried as he re-entered the kitchen.

Peter gaped. 'Have I missed something?'

'Hello, Peter.' Hal held out a hand. 'Sorry to infiltrate, but the girls needed a bit of help'.

Peter automatically shook hands. 'And why was that?'

'We got caught out in the storm.'

'What storm?' Kathleen and Peter spoke together.

'You two have been fast asleep, haven't you?' Jennifer said.

'Well, yes.' Kathleen poured boiling water into a large teapot. 'I'd just got up when you arrived.'

'I did say not to go too far, I thought we might get a drop of rain.'

Hal smiled. 'I think you could say

we've had a drop.'

Peter moved to the window. 'Seems so, puddles everywhere.'

'The lanes were flooded so Hal gave us a lift home.'

'From where?'

There was a taut little silence.

'Ellie and I were sheltering in the barn . . . on the other side of Keeper's Copse.'

Kathleen drew in a sharp breath. Her fingers holding the milk jug turned white at the knuckles.

'The barn was the only place to shelter.'

'The girls were already there when I turned up to get out of the rain.'

Kathleen took a deep breath and continued to pour out the teas. 'Can't remember if you take sugar, Hal.'

'No thanks, Mrs Dunbar.'

She passed him a mug. 'I'm glad to have both of them back safely. Thanks.'

'Well, I considered letting them paddle home,' he said, lightening the situation, 'but I thought, no, be a shame to get the pushchair rusty.'

'Good job you went into the barn, lad,' Peter said, gulping hot tea appreciatively.

'With his horse,' Ellie piped up, taking time off from drinking orange juice through a straw. 'An', d'you know,' she took another long suck, 'he kissed Auntie Jen.' She nodded firmly. 'He did. He kissed her in the barn.'

5

The two men had disappeared to their respective work: Hal to the farm and Peter down to the stables.

Kathleen was peeling potatoes in readiness for the evening meal. 'I've never known Ellie tell a fib,' she said smiling broadly. 'So my nose is definitely itching.'

'Why am I not surprised?' Jennifer finished rolling chunks of raw beef in seasoned flour and slid them into the hot oil to seal.

'You're saying I'm nosy?'

'No, you did.'

Kathleen laughed. 'Oh come on, Jennifer love . . . '

'Really, there's nothing to tell.'

'I remember you saying, 'Ask me again when I've met him' . . . '

'Hmm, yes, I did. But truly, the embers are not being fanned.'

Kathleen concentrated her gaze on the half-peeled potato in her hand as she tried to hide her disappointment.

'Sorry, Mum, you see it was Ellie who insisted Hal give me a kiss because she'd already planted one of her really big sloppy ones. I was crying and she was playing at little mummy. She's such a sweet-natured tot, she was kissing me better. Then, of course, she pressured Hal — 'Just to make sure,' she said and well . . . he kissed me.'

'I see.'

They carried on preparing the food, the only sound in the kitchen the sizzling hot oil.

'Actually, no, I don't see.' Kathleen drained off the starchy water in the potato saucepan and refilled it with fresh. 'I've just realised you said you were crying. What was wrong?'

Jennifer's thoughts squirreled round inside her head. She could hardly say because of the precious memories of making love to Hal in that same barn only to lose him, followed by the tearing grief of losing Rosamund.

'I guess I was thinking about Rosamund.'

'Darling,' Kathleen came over and put her arms around Jennifer. 'You're bound to choke up now and again, your father and I both do.'

Jennifer felt a heel. It was all she could do not to come clean and admit that half of the grief was because of Hal. Their love had been far beyond the usual depth of feeling. She'd felt his loss like the amputation of a vital organ. But if she admitted this, Kathleen would get her hopes up again. And there was no point because inevitably they would be dashed down.

'It's hard for all of us, Mum, we have to remember the good times. Rosamund would want us to.'

'Absolutely.' Kathleen fished a tissue from her pinny pocket and had a strong blow. 'It would be better not to go anywhere near Keeper's Copse or the barn. I can't imagine why you walked so far, not very sensible was it?'

Jennifer briefly considered defending herself but she was tired. The emotions of the day had left her drained. So she merely shook her head. Suddenly all she wanted was to escape to her bedroom, lie down on the familiar comforting bed and let the tensions flow away, maybe even have a short nap.

Stirring the beef chunks she tipped them out into the warmed casserole dish. 'All yours, Mum, ready for the root veg.' On the point of adding she was going upstairs, a wailing siren could be heard turning off the main road and entering their lane.

Both women stared at each other.

'Ambulance?'

Jennifer nodded. 'Sounds like it.' The siren grew louder. Both women realised at the same moment that it was headed for Swallow House Stables.

Kathleen's face turned white. Her fingers clutched the edge of the sink. 'Peter . . . ?'

Jennifer swallowed hard. 'Wait here,

Mum, I'll go and find out what's happened.'

'No, no, I'm coming.'

'No you're not.' Jennifer's voice was firm. 'Look after Ellie.' Without waiting for a reply she hastened out the back door and ran across to the stables.

The ambulance swung into the yard and abruptly cut the siren. The silence following seemed equally as loud as the noise had been a split second before.

The door to the tack room was open and Jennifer ran in. Will Banbury was lying on a horse rug spread over the floor with a further rug covering him. His eyes were squeezed tightly closed, sweat beading his forehead. It didn't need guesswork to know he was in great pain. Peter was hunkered down beside him folding a wet cloth into a flat strip. He glanced up as Jennifer came in.

'Here, lass, hold this against his forehead. I'll go and fetch the ambulance chaps.'

'What happened?'

But her father was already out of the

door. She laid the cold cloth on Will's glistening forehead.

He expelled a deep breath. 'Aaaah, that's good.' But it was said through clenched teeth.

'Pain's bad, yes?'

'You could say.'

'Don't talk, then. The ambulance has just arrived. They'll give you something for the pain.'

A few moments later Jennifer was being moved aside as two uniformed men deposited a medical bag beside the injured man.

She went outside to join Peter as they waited for the diagnosis.

'He got kicked.' Peter shook his head. 'Took it straight on the kneecap. It's certain to be dislocated, possibly broken.'

'Which horse?'

'Would you believe, Popeye?'

'Yes,' Jennifer grimaced. 'Yes, I would believe it. He's got a mean streak.'

'Sent Will over backwards, reckon he got a nasty crack on the back of his head, too. He was out cold for a couple of minutes. That's when I rang for an ambulance.'

'You could have fetched me to help . . . '

'No time. I needed to get him out of the stable, away from the horse.'

'Good job Popeye's in the last stable.'

'Hmmm, that's what I thought.'

One of the ambulance men appeared in the open doorway. 'Going to have to take him to the Queen's,' he said, referring to the massive hospital in Nottingham.

'Anything I can do?' Peter offered.

'No thanks, we'll just stretcher him into the ambulance. He needs X-rays on his head and knee.'

'I'd better send one of the other lads with him, then.' Peter glanced round the yard and beckoned to Joe.

'I'll go if you like,' Jennifer offered.

'I want you here, lass, to do Will's horses.'

She swallowed a sigh of regret for the loss of a much-needed break and the workload now facing her. But looking at Will's face, contorted with pain, as he was carried past on the stretcher into the ambulance, made her own needs feel insignificant.

They watched as Joe hopped up into the ambulance and the man closed the doors.

'I reckon he'll be lucky if it's not broken his kneecap.' Peter chewed his bottom lip. 'Whatever the verdict, he'll be out of action for a while.' He clapped a hand on Jennifer's shoulder. 'That leaves me a jockey short for tomorrow's race at Leicester.' He raised an eyebrow. 'So, how about it?'

Suddenly the exhaustion fell away. 'You want me to ride Dixie?'

'If you want to.'

She hugged him tight. 'I want to. Thanks, Dad.'

'You won't be thanking me in a minute because Will was just about to feed Popeye when he got laid out. And with the sound of it, waiting for his feed hasn't improved his temper.'

Jennifer could hear the stamp of an impatient hoof and the shrill whinny coming from Popeye's stable.

'Oh well, there's always two sides to the same coin.' She reached for a feed bucket.

'Oh, and Jennifer . . . '

'Yes?'

'Watch yourself. As you so rightly said, he has a mean streak.' Starting to walk away, he stopped and swung round, 'Funny, isn't it. He's like a new born lamb with our Ellie.'

Jennifer hefted the bucket. 'She's special.'

'Aye, indeed she is.' He smiled at her and strode away across the stable yard.

* * *

The next morning Jennifer was up before six o'clock. Standing in the kitchen, sipping a hot coffee laced with honey for energy, she was aware of a thrill running through her. It felt so good to be back in the saddle

— literally, in another few minutes — and an involuntary grin spread over her face. But her ever-vigilant conscience reminded her she was supposed to be helping with Ellie and guilt took over.

'I could just ride out first lot, Mum, and be back in time for Ellie's breakfast. What do you think?'

'I think you should get yourself outside and help your father.'

'But I won't have chance to pull my weight with her later because I'm racing this afternoon.'

Kathleen smiled. 'And I'm so glad. I want you to enjoy your life, Jennifer, and racing is your life. I can easily manage the tot today. You'll be here to help with her dinner tonight and she'll be so pleased after not seeing you all day, she might even eat it without cribbing. So, get yourself off outside and get some horses looked after.'

'Love you, Mum, thanks.' Jennifer gave her quick kiss.

'What's that for?'

'Bashing my guilt complex on the head.'

* * *

Down in the stables there was no time to think about Ellie nor any possible guilt twinges. With a lad away and two horses scheduled for afternoon races, it was down to work and keep going. Swallow House Stables was a fairly small yard with the minimum of staff to run it. The dividing line between horses and the number of lads to look after them financially was a thin one. A very necessary one if the business was to continue as a viable concern. Years ago it would have been a 3 to 1 ratio; now it could easily be 5 or more. It was a tough life for stable lads, which also included girls, but that was exactly what it was — not simply a job, but a way of life.

After mucking out and grooming, Jennifer tacked up her first horse, Above the Horizon. With iron shod hooves clattering, she led him out into the yard. Two or three of the other lads were also out walking their horses in tight circles, waiting to swing up into the saddles and ride out in single file down the lane to the gallops.

There was the usual banter and leg-pulling, Jennifer as the newcomer, despite being the boss's daughter, getting the brunt of it.

'These part-timers y'know,' Stevie said, kicking on Golden Girl, 'they just can't hack it.'

'Oh trot off,' Jennifer responded, laughing. 'And I'm supposed to be riding upsides with you, don't forget. Horizon will leave you standing.'

Peter, having given out the riding instructions earlier, had taken the Land Rover to the mid-point of the gallops and parked up with his field glasses trained on the string.

Although there was friendly rivalry between the lads, once they'd reached the gallops, it was serious work riding. Stevie and Jennifer as back-markers, waited until the rest of the string had cantered away before shortening their reins and kicking on.

As she always did, Jennifer felt a great surge of joy as Above the Horizon lengthened his stride and the green turf flashed away beneath his pounding hooves. The wind rushing against her face was cool, cleansing, and she knew this was her rightful work. So many people struggled on doing nine to five jobs they hated and had to endure. And here she was, on a glorious summer morning doing a job that did not feel like work at all. To do something you loved that provided your living was indeed a blessing. She was so very lucky.

Riding spoke to her inner self and she felt complete harmony with her horse. Gripping with her calves and knees, she stood in the stirrups, her body moving in absolute accord with the powerful animal that was rapidly eating up the ground headed for the end of the gallops.

As predicted, Above the Horizon proved the fastest and beat Golden Girl by a full two lengths. She pulled back to a blowing trot and then walked him over to meet Peter who had driven down to the end.

'He's entered next week at the Nottingham meeting with Will riding and on this morning's showing he should do well. However, since Joe's told me Will's kneecap's broken, afraid that's him out for six weeks at least. So, do you want all his rides?'

'Sorry about Will, what rotten bad luck for him,' Jennifer said. 'But yes,' a wide grin spread across her face, 'if Mum can cope with Ellie, I'd love the rides.'

* * *

'We've made good time,' Mike, the travelling head lad said. Turning the wheel of the massive horse box, he took a right off the A46 roundabout, down the straight and an immediate left towards the horse box park. Race-goers were streaming along the approach to the racecourse turnstiles, their spirits and optimism on an infectious high. The atmosphere was one of cheerful excitement.

Jennifer had packed the racing bag the previous evening and now dumped it off at the racecourse stables on route before Mike drove on to find a space to park the horse box. Leicester was a popular Midland venue and horses declared in the earlier races had already arrived. Everywhere was bustle and activity.

The mobile vans dispensing fast food were in full production. Delicious tantalising smells from fish and chips to baked potatoes with curry sauce to hot dogs and fried onions drifted across, tickling taste-buds. Race-goers who had travelled long distances were taking advantage and trade was brisk. Queues were long for coffee and tea.

Jennifer took a deep appreciative breath. The more immediate smell was of hot horse but the other smells permeated as well and coalesced into familiar, yet exhilarating satisfaction. All the people here were out for a day's pleasure and the positivity was practically tangible.

But there was little time to spend appreciating the ambience. There were two horses boxed up that had to be attended and taken to the stables. From there they would then await their turn to be led to the saddling boxes edging the pre-parade ring. Thirty minutes before their allotted race they'd be led to the parade ring. This ring was always thronged around, probably six deep, with race-goers all keen to see their particular choice being walked round. Dixie was racing in the three-thirty with Morning Cloud an hour later.

By three-fifteen Jennifer was in the jockey's changing room already changed into the owner's, Mrs Cuthbertson's, colours of pink and navy blue stripes. There were eight runners altogether and Jennifer knew most of the jockeys. But it gave her a jolt when one of them approached her.

'Hiya, didn't expect to see you here.' It was one of the lads from Jackson's yard in Lambourn.

'Filling in, Dad's jockey got kicked in the stable last night.'

The lad looked at her sideways, 'One of your dad's is it?'

'Yes.' Jennifer, feeling the colour rise in her cheeks, bent down to pull on a racing boot, glad of the chance to look away from his searching gaze.

'Busman's holiday, innit? You was supposed to be on holiday.'

'Yes, well, Dad's short staffed so I'm helping out.'

'You *are* coming back to Jackson's, aren't you?'

Jennifer gave a final tug to the boot as the outside bell rang signalling all the jockeys to the parade ring to mount up.

'I've two weeks off, right.'

'Sure.' He turned away and followed the rest out into the bright sunshine.

Jennifer heaved a sigh of relief and

took a further couple of deep breaths to calm the butterflies. Always before a race, her stomach fluttered with nerves but it also gave her a charge of adrenalin, something she was convinced helped to put the extra edge on her riding. But it had been very bad luck meeting that jockey. All it needed was for him to return to Lambourn, mention the meeting, and she'd have Jackson on the telephone. This could be the push that forced her hand. It was decision time now.

She hurried after the pack and scanned the parade ring for Stevie who was leading round Dixie. Slipping through the crowd clustered around the entrance, she went up to Dixie and slapped his neck before accepting Stevie's help in legging her up into the minuscule racing saddle. All the jockeys were now mounted and she rode after them in a parade of brilliantly coloured silks.

The leading horse angled out of the ring and, practically tugging the lad off his feet, headed down the tarmac path and out onto the racecourse. The rest of the horses and jockeys followed. Jennifer felt the change in Dixie as his hooves met turf and experienced the thrill that ran through his rippling muscles as she allowed him to break into a canter.

They were on their way and the starting stalls were waiting.

6

The grandfather clock in the cottage was striking seven o'clock when Jennifer entered the kitchen, bone-weary but triumphant. She'd already received a congratulatory pat on the shoulder from her father as she was settling Dixie down for the night in the stable.

'Well done, lass, I thought he was ready for that race. Next time we'll enter him for a high class race.'

'Morning Cloud made a fair showing, too. Marcus is a useful jockey, he rode a pretty good race.' Morning Cloud had come third in the later race.

'Will came out of hospital today. Orders are to lay-up. He's really sick about it but he knows his job's still here for him. I do reckon though, we need another lad on the team. You know anyone who might suit?'

'Not off-hand but I think you're

right. We seem a bit stretched.'

'Aye, and I'll tell you something else lass, I've heard today we're getting all Redfern's new horses in a couple of months.'

'Wow, that's really great news. We shall definitely need more staff.' She frowned. 'Talking about jobs, I have to make a quick decision about my future, Dad.' She told him about meeting the lad in the changing room.

'When Jackson hears, he'll know which way the smoke's blowing. You'd best have your answer ready, our Jennifer.'

'I could use your impartial advice.'

He looked at her steadily. 'Try considering you've no choice. It's useful to turn it upside down — gets your emotional reactions working rather than just using your logic. How do you feel about going back permanently to Lambourn?'

'Thanks, Dad. I'll give it a go.' She would need to be relaxed and on her own first.

Now, in the kitchen patting the fussy retriever that was pressing against her legs, she braced herself as Ellie, who had heard her voice, hurtled into the room. Freshly bathed, dressed in a pink nightie with golden curls dancing round her face, she looked cherubic. She gave a whoop of delight and threw herself into Jennifer's arms.

'Hello, angel, my what a welcome. Have you missed me?'

Ellie let go. Unable to contain her exuberance, she jumped up and down. 'Yes, yes, yes!'

'Steady,' Jennifer laughed. 'You'll never get off to sleep.'

'Read me a story, Auntie Jen.' The child stood still and gazed up at Jennifer with enormous pleading eyes. They were filled with love and they melted Jennifer's heart.

'You bet, my angel. Just let me wash my hands first.'

'Well done.' Kathleen came into the kitchen. 'What better homecoming than to ride your first horse in as a winner.'

She hurried to make a mug of tea. 'There you are, you can drink and read at the same time.'

Bending down she picked up the little girl. 'Come on, let's get you snuggled up in bed.'

'Can I choose my story?'

''Course you can,' Kathleen dropped a kiss on her cheek, 'but it will have to be a short one 'cos your Auntie Jen's very tired tonight.'

'She's been riding hard.' Ellie emphasised her observation with a firm nod.

'Out of the mouths of babes,' Jennifer agreed laughing as she followed them up the twisty staircase.

* * *

Much later in the bathroom, following a delicious hot dinner of flavoursome chicken stew, Jennifer lowered herself thankfully into a deep bath of steamy bubbles. Adjusting the bath cushion behind her head, she stretched out in the perfumed water and let go of the day's accumulated tensions. She was tired but it was a pleasant, natural tiredness borne of an early start, being out in the fresh air and hard physical work.

Closing her eyes, she re-lived the highlights of the day and knew her life to be satisfyingly good. Imprinting the race on her mind, she added to the visual memory of winning all the scents and feelings she had experienced during those two minutes. It was so important to have a positive mindset she could draw on when she needed it ready for her next race. Having committed it to memory, she blessed all her experiences that day.

The warm water was so soothing, it was all she could do to stay awake. But there was one thing she must do before retiring to an early bed. Her father's advice was sound as she'd known it would be. She allowed her thoughts to wander back to Lambourn and her life down there. Thinking about the day she was due back, she imagined herself walking into Jackson's stable yard, suitcase in hand and unlocking her flat door. As she mentally opened the door she envisaged living there permanently. How did the visualization affect her emotionally?

She'd be her own person, no-one else to consider, every decision her own. Yes, it was attractive. But every time she returned from work it would be to an empty flat. Who needed her there? She contrasted it with her homecoming today as she walked in at the kitchen door. An immediate welcome from the happy dog closely followed by the ecstatic welcome from Ellie and loving support given unconditionally from her mother. There was no comparison.

She climbed out of the bath, wrapped herself in a warm white towel and padded down the landing to her bedroom.

Picking up the telephone she dialled Jackson's number.

* * *

If she had had any doubts about her decision, driving home two weeks later after working her notice, they were dispelled before she even reached Swallow House Stables. An uprush of loving anticipation had started the minute she'd dropped off the keys to her flat in Lambourn. Now as the miles fled away behind her, the emotion continued to grow.

Just once before leaving to work her notice, she'd bumped into Hal in the local supermarket.

'Stocking up?' He'd grinned over a promotional stack of tins partially blocking the aisle.

'Oh, hello.' She'd angled the shopping trolley around the stack. 'I am, actually. I'm on my way to work for my Governor, Mr Jackson, in Lambourn.'

His face saddened. 'You've decided against staying at home, then? Well,' he sighed, 'I can't say I'm pleased with your choice because it would surely make me a liar. But, if it's right for you . . . ' his voice tailed away.

'No, you've got it wrong. I'm going because it's only fair I should work my notice.'

His eyes brightened. 'You're coming back again?'

'Yes, this is where I'm most needed.'

'Indeed it is, Jenny.' His eyes were saying more than his lips.

'Have to press on.' She grabbed three of the cut price tins and piled them into the trolley.

The smile was still on his face. 'I'm glad we met.'

'So am I.' And she realised she was, ridiculously so. She hesitated. 'There's actually something I wanted to ask you, Hal. Do you remember when we were in the barn . . . ?'

'Yes, I do.' His smile broadened.

Overwhelming embarrassment flooded through her. 'I was referring to the last time, when I was saying about wanting to try and track down Ellie's father.'

'Yes, you were most emphatic about it.'

'And I still am. It's very important to

me and, of course, to Ellie's future. Well, I was thinking about it last night, knowing it has to be shelved until my return. It was too late then to ring you but I wondered if you could have a word with your sister for me?'

'Anya?'

'Hmmm . . . '

'But how could she possibly help?'

'I remembered Rosamund was in her class at school. Do you think you could ask Anya if she'd mind me having a chat with her?'

'I'll certainly ask her. It's not the most social life she leads up at the farm. I'm sure she'd welcome the chance to see a new face. But as to whether it will help you . . . I don't really think so.'

'But you will ask her?'

'Oh, sure.'

'Look, I do have to go. I'll ring you when I get back from Lambourn.'

'OK.'

* * *

Turning into Swallow House Stable yard, she parked the Mini, switched off the engine and sat quite still. She was seeing it, albeit familiar, as if for the first time. The emotion changed from anticipation to a deeply satisfying sense of belonging.

It was going to mean a juggling act to pursue her career in race riding and pull her weight in Ellie's upbringing but she'd simply have to pace herself. Other women faced tough odds as they battled to do right by their families and children and still managed to hold down demanding jobs. She'd be no different. The only difference was Ellie wasn't her natural born child.

As the thought came so too did the cold feeling inside and the knowledge that she could never give birth to a baby of her own. She pressed the unwelcome feeling down deep inside. It would never go away, never leave her. How could it? The unalterable fact was she was barren.

Many times it had overwhelmed her

bringing despair and wild tears. But at no time had it had greater effect than when Rosamund died. In one stroke, her death had deprived Ellie — already sentenced to no cousins in her life — of any chance of a sibling. Not only was Ellie left as a single child in the family, but Kathleen and Peter had lost any chance of becoming grandparents again. And that irrevocable fact caused pain.

Jennifer was eaten by guilt, irrational guilt since there was nothing she could do about her condition. Yet it still left her feeling their sorrow was her own fault.

The sound of knuckles rapping against the car window jerked her back to the present moment. She hastily lowered the window.

'You going to stay there all day?' Peter bent to look at her. 'Your mum's struggling, you know. Little 'un had her up three times last night.'

Her guilt changed from inadequate self-image to guilt from dereliction of duty. But this type was easily remedied.

She sloughed off the enervating negativity. 'Sorry, Dad, I was miles away.'

'Aye, well, you're home now, lass.' His voice softened and he looked concerned. 'You are pleased to be back, aren't you? Only, you don't look happy.'

She slid from the car and gave him a long hug. 'I'm home, and I'm happy.'

* * *

For a few nights Ellie slept soundly. Then came the night the child's screams awoke Jennifer in the early hours. The word juggling ran through her sleep-befuddled brain. She was away racing today at Newmarket and a broken night's sleep was definitely not what she needed. But nor was it what her mother needed. The noise was sure to wake her, too.

Jumping out of bed, she hurried to Ellie's room. She was, amazingly, still asleep, but clutching in torment at empty air.

Jennifer lifted the duvet and slid into bed, stroking the child's cheek. She allowed Ellie to grab hold of her hand. The reaction was immediate. The wails ceased abruptly. At first Ellie clung to it like a lifeline, and then the rigid little body lying next to her relaxed. Just one whispered word was audible, 'Mummy . . . ' Ellie curled her body trustingly against Jennifer. She was still fast asleep.

Pondering on the chances of being able to climb out of bed without waking the tot, Jennifer decided it wasn't worth the risk. Ellie was resting peacefully now but still holding onto her hand. If she tried to disentangle herself it might prove disastrous. Surrendering to the warm soft bed, Jennifer drifted off to sleep as well.

7

'You've had a phone call.' Kathleen raised an eyebrow and looked arch.

'Don't tell me.' Jennifer toed off her boots at the kitchen door. She was tired and it was only half-past twelve but with a six o'clock start behind her, that still added up to more than six hours' hard physical work. 'Now who in the world could put that look on your face? Let me guess. Oh yes, would his name be Hal?'

'Dead right.' Her mother continued mixing a large bowl of assorted salad.

'Now why doesn't that surprise me?'

'Less cheek, if you please.'

Jennifer relented. 'I just wish you'd stop matchmaking. It's not going to happen. Anyway, what did he say?'

'He invited you round on Sunday afternoon. Said he appreciated you'd be busy all the rest of the week.'

It was Jennifer's turn to raise an eyebrow. 'Why on earth should he want to see me?'

'He mentioned Anya.'

'Oh, yes, of course,' Jennifer nodded, 'I remember now. I told him I'd ring to arrange a convenient time when I got back from Lambourn. With everything going on, I'd forgotten.'

'So, are you going to tell me about it?'

'Nothing to tell. I remembered Rosamund was in the same class at school as Anya. It's a very slim chance that she might know something but I thought I'd give it a go and ask her.'

'About?'

'About who Ellie's father might be.'

Kathleen dropped the salad spoon. 'Oh no, Jennifer, it might stir up all sorts of implications. We can manage fine now you've come home. Far better to let things lie.'

'Mum, somewhere out there is Ellie's father. It's his duty to share in her life.'

'I don't see why. We've managed so

far, we can go on doing it.'

'OK, maybe whilst Rosamund was alive it wasn't an issue. At least Ellie had one parent. But now she's gone — that makes Ellie an orphan.'

'We don't need him.' Kathleen's lips tightened. 'Ellie's got us.'

'But he's her own flesh and blood, too. I mean, Rosamund wasn't promiscuous, she must have been in love with the man, or at least thought she was.' This was the first time she'd spoken her mind about Rosamund. To begin with the grief of her loss had been too intense. It had taken several months to be able to talk as objectively and openly as this. 'It's obvious he wasn't in love with her, but . . . '

'You can't say that.' Kathleen rinsed the salad spoon under the hot tap. 'He may very well have been.'

Jennifer stared at her mother. 'Well, if he was, why didn't he stand up and support her.'

'I don't know . . . I've always assumed he must have been a married man.'

'And that absolves him, does it?'

'No, of course not.' Kathleen said unhappily. 'But think of all the trouble it will cause if you do find out who he is.'

Jennifer continued to stare at her mother. A horrid feeling was growing inside her. 'You know who he is, don't you?' she whispered.

'I do not! How can you say such a thing.' Kathleen's face had gone white.

'But you *think* you know, don't you?'

'I . . . I might have my suspicions, yes, but that's not the same thing.'

'Did Rosamund give you any indication who it was?'

'No.'

'But she did say something, didn't she?' Jennifer probed. 'She must have done to give you an impression of who it might be.'

'Rosamund said she had her own self-respect,' Kathleen's voice was low, 'and she wasn't going to risk jeopardising other people's lives, or risk being pitied. Truly, Jennifer, she didn't say anything more about him.'

'You've never told me that before.'

'No, well,' Kathleen turned away and began to set the table for lunch, 'that's why I don't think it's a good idea for you to go digging about and bringing things to light.'

'You think it might harm Rosamund's memory?'

'Not in our eyes, Jennifer, we're her family. But it's possible it might alter the way other people remember her.'

'Mum,' Jennifer put her arms around her, 'please don't get upset. Rosamund was a lovely person, everybody thought so. They all seemed to be on her side when she became pregnant. Nobody blamed her. They were all gunning for the guilty man.'

Kathleen tore off a square of kitchen paper and blew her nose hard. 'I know they were. And I'd rather leave it at that, Jennifer. Promise me you won't go stirring things up.'

'I can't do that, Mum, I'm sorry. There's Ellie's future involved here. She has rights, too. One day she's going to ask who her father is.'

'I know she is, but if we can't tell her, that's all there is to it.'

'Mum,' Jennifer bit her lip, 'I promise not to upset the apple-cart, but can't you just tell me who you think it is?'

'It wouldn't be right. And I'm not going to.' Angrily, she clattered cutlery onto the kitchen table. 'I want you to promise to let well alone.'

Sandy suddenly jumped up, tail wagging, as Peter came into the kitchen.

Despite her mother's strong feelings, Jennifer wasn't about to promise and now with Peter's presence, the moment had passed. She felt relieved she'd been reprieved from answering.

'I'll just go and give Hal a ring, confirm I'll go up Sunday afternoon.'

'You two getting together again?' Peter enquired.

'Long story, Dad, but no, not in the way you think.'

He turned back to the sink and resumed washing his hands. 'Pity.'

* * *

Jennifer used the phone in her own room and it was picked up on the third ring.

'Hello, Anya Taylor speaking.'

Jennifer, having mentally prepared herself to speak to Hal, was momentarily wrong-footed. 'Oh, hello, this is Jennifer, from Swallow House.'

'How nice to hear from you.' Anya's voice held genuine warmth. 'Hal mentioned he'd seen you. Are you glad to be back home again?'

'Yes, yes I am, very glad.'

'That's great. Can you make it this Sunday?'

'Yes, I was ringing to make it definite. About two o'clock, do you think?'

'Anytime, really, but I suppose it would be best around then. Mum will have had her lunch and she usually has a little sleep afterwards so we can chat undisturbed.'

'Sounds fine, as long as I'm not being a nuisance.'

'Goodness no, we hardly get a visitor from one month's end to the next. It will be lovely to see you.'

'Do you mind if I ask some questions? I have to be honest, Anya, it's not just a social call.'

'Jennifer, if you knew how down right bored I get never seeing anyone, you wouldn't even ask.'

'OK then, I'll look forward to seeing you Sunday.'

'Me, too.'

She replaced the phone and sat thinking about the conversation.

Anya was a good deal younger, probably about six years. She couldn't really remember noticing her at school. As Hal's sister, yes, sometimes their age groups had mixed on special outings or celebrations, but six years difference at that age was a far different gap than when adult.

Anya had seemed genuinely pleased she had made contact and Jennifer realised that although Anya had said how isolated she was up at the farm, she herself had no close girlfriends. Apart from the question of Ellie's parentage, it would make a lovely change to chat with another girl of about her own age. She could chat with her mother, of course, but it wasn't quite the same thing.

She found she was really looking forward to Sunday.

* * *

'I know I'm only a man,' Peter began, 'but am I allowed to know why Jennifer's giving young Hal the cold shoulder?'

'I wish I could give you an answer. It makes no sense to me.'

'I don't reckon there's another woman, I mean, it struck me the other day, he was only waiting for her to crook a finger.'

'Yes,' Kathleen sighed and set the plates out on the table, 'I got the same impression.'

'Do you reckon I could have a word

with her. P'raps after the bust-up they had, she might think he's not interested.'

'Oh no, Peter, she's a woman and she *knows* he's interested.'

'Well . . . it beats me.'

'Maybe she's playing hard to get. Although, I don't really think she is. If you're asking my opinion, I'd say she's still got strong feelings for Hal. But for some reason, she's doing her best to get along without him.'

'Whatever the reason,' he tapped the side of his nose, 'and there has to be a strong reason, she must think it serious enough to keep them apart.'

'She's going round to the farm on Sunday but it's not to see Hal, it's to speak to Anya. Oh, Peter, she's going to quiz that poor girl about who Ellie's father might be.'

'Why should she know anything?'

'Apparently Anya was in the same class at school as Rosamund.'

'Even so, I don't see why. It's a good four years ago, life changes, people move on. Even if she did have girlie chats with Rosamund, I don't suppose she'd remember anything relevant.'

'Well, let's hope you're right.'

Peter gave her a searching look. 'Do I take it you'd rather not find out who this man is?'

Kathleen gripped the edge of the table tightly. 'You're asking me directly so, yes, I hope Jennifer can't find out his identity.'

Peter put a strong hand over hers where it lay on the table. 'Steady on, Kathleen, me duck. Let's get this straight; you've said many a time you wondered who it could be, you can't deny that. Now, suddenly, since Jennifer's taken up the cause — and it will be for the highest motive, knowing our Jennifer — you don't want her to find out. Now why? What are you afraid of?'

Kathleen leaned against his broad chest and drew strength from him. 'I'm so very afraid she will discover for definite who he is.'

'Are you trying to tell me you already

suspect someone?'

'Logically, no, it can't possibly be him.'

'For goodness sake, woman, who?'

But Kathleen shook her head mulishly. 'I'm just being silly.'

He let it go and said, 'But if she does find out what are you afraid of?'

'Don't you see, Peter, Rosamund's death has changed everything. If Jennifer does track him down, he will be Ellie's next of kin. By law, he could claim her, take her away. You should be afraid, too.' She tugged at his shirt in agitation. 'We could lose her.'

'Oh my God.' He stared at her in shock. 'I never thought of that.'

* * *

At half past one on Sunday, Jennifer went upstairs and changed into a dress. It was the first time in weeks, months, she'd worn anything other than trousers.

She slipped on the pale grey jersey

and checked her appearance in the mirror. The dress fitted beautifully, which told her she had lost a lot of weight since she'd last worn it, two Christmases ago. But since then she'd split up with Hal and Rosamund had died. Both traumas had caused the weight to fall off her. Not that she'd been fat to start with. All the hard physical slog of her day-to-day life ensured that.

Standing in front of the mirror she loosened the scrunchie holding back her hair and brushed it in long sweeps. The waves tumbled over her shoulders in a shining fall of auburn. Suddenly, she was aware of herself as an attractive woman — attractive enough to interest men. She sighed and dropped the hairbrush back onto the dressing table. When they realised she was infertile, they'd run.

Besides, there was only one man she was interested in. She sucked in a sharp breath. She'd actually admitted it to herself. Hal was the only man for her.

However, because of the past situation, she knew where his true loyalties lay and it was hopeless to waste her life hoping he would change. She mentally shook herself. Daydreaming wouldn't get her very far, life was for getting on with.

Catching up the Mini keys from her bedside cabinet, she headed downstairs.

* * *

The aromatic smell of cinnamon filled her nostrils. Jennifer sniffed appreciatively as she entered the farmhouse kitchen. 'Something smells gorgeous.'

Anya smiled. 'Mother likes it added to apple pie.'

'Thanks very much for letting me come interrupting you. I know you have your hands full.'

Anya grinned. 'Us multi-tasking women need to stick together.'

Jennifer smiled back. 'How true.'

'Do come through to the sitting room.'

Nothing appeared to have changed since she had been here before. Tastefully decorated in shades of soft green, it offered a calm relaxing oasis in the midst of busy farm life.

'How about a cup of tea?'

'Hmmm, yes, please.'

Anya returned to the kitchen and Jennifer wandered to the bookshelves that lined one wall. She remembered Hal was a great reader. They had bantered about the merits of the books they had read, chosen a title and each read a copy to compare later. A sharp stab of loss for the shared mental level of their relationship pierced through her. Theirs had never been solely a physical attraction. She had enjoyed discussions on deeper issues with him as well as the lighter fun-filled aspects of simply being together. This room, the whole farm, was so filled with his personality it was almost tangible.

'Here we are.' Anya angled the tray through the door. 'Tea up.' She'd added a plate of cinnamon shortcake and as

Jennifer sampled a finger she was impressed by what a good cook Anya was.

'Do you have a job apart from looking after your mother and running the farmhouse?'

'Not really,' Anya sighed. 'I'd love a career, well, who wouldn't? I do Hal's farm paperwork for him and I'm afraid there's masses of it. Farming's not like it used to be.'

'No, I'm sure.'

'But I'm not free enough to take an outside-based job. Mother needs some-one round in the house.'

'It must be difficult. You must get frustrated.'

'I do, actually,' Anya confessed. 'I've not said anything to Hal about how I really feel. But Hal's so busy with the physical work on the farm, it would be impossible for him to see to Mother.'

'Is there no hope of her getting any better?'

'I think it would take a miracle.' The

sadness in the girl's face moved Jennifer.

'They *do* happen, sometimes.'

'She never got over losing Father, you see.'

'Yes, Hal said.'

Anya leaned forward earnestly, 'He does care for you, Jennifer. What caused the rift between you? Is there no chance . . . ?'

Jennifer looked down at her cup and shook her head. How could she say Anya herself was part of the problem, not to mention Mrs Taylor. Hal's commitment to his family and the future of the farm, in his family for generations, was deep and whilst she applauded his loyalty, it gave no space for herself and her own needs.

Anya flapped her hands. 'Look, please, forget I mentioned it, OK? Let's enjoy your visit. It's ages since I had a visitor and the chance of a change of conversation.'

Jennifer sighed with relief. Anya was a sweet girl. No way would she say anything that might hurt her.

'Tell me, you said it wasn't a social call as such, what is it you wanted to ask me?'

'You knew my sister, Rosamund. Were you a friend of hers?'

'She was in my class at school, yes, we were pretty friendly. I'm dreadfully sorry she died. She was very popular, you know, at school.'

'I wondered if you could tell me about her circle of friends, not only at school but perhaps local people as well?'

'We both went to a young farmers group now and again and, of course, the youth club, over at Whatton in the Vale. And at weekends we were co-helpers on the 'Saturday Give Back,' too.'

'Oh yes, I can remember that starting up,' Jennifer nodded. 'Fourth formers and onwards were allowed to join, weren't they?'

'That's right. We'd go out on a roster basis to elderly residents, see if there were any odd jobs we could help with. Mainly it was pinning up and taking down washing, walking dogs, shopping, that kind of thing. We'd get friendly with some of the elderly people's relatives as well, those living away from the village who could only call in occasionally on their parents.'

Jennifer felt her confidence start to slip. It would seem Rosamund's friends stretched from here to Australia. The possibility of finding the right one seemed even more remote than when she'd begun.

'Do you recall Rosamund getting friendly with any older men?'

'Well, yes, she may have done but if so she kept it quiet because I can't think of anyone special.'

'Do you know if she kept up any visiting after she left school?'

'I don't, no. The one old lady she was very in tune with was Maud from Porters' Row cottages. They seemed to get on really well. I've known Rosamund to call round on other days apart from Saturday. Mainly, I think she used to read to the old lady because Maud's eye-sight wasn't too good. But as to anyone else, I'm afraid I can't help, sorry.'

'No, you have helped, an awful lot. With the age difference between us, obviously, I wasn't doing the same things as she was.'

'I remember there were seven or eight of us at school who palled around together. If we went over to Nottingham for a night out say, or a pop concert, some of our brothers and sisters might join in.' She laughed. 'The girls developed crushes, some went off in twosomes, you know how it is.'

'Did Rosamund have a crush on any particular boy?' Jennifer mentally crossed her fingers.

'Not that I can think of. A gang of us went to the Theatre Royal to see a pop group, all us girls were madly in love with the lead singer. Not that we pelted him with our knickers, so it wasn't Tom Jones.' They both giggled.

'I must have gone through that stage,' Jennifer grinned, 'but I can't remember ever flinging knickers myself.'

'I tell you what we did do, though, after the show, we went round to the stage door and queued for ages to get his autograph.'

'Did Rosamund?'

'Oh yes. We must have been mad when you think back, because I can't for the life of me remember his name.'

'You probably threw them away a month or two later.'

'Now that's where you're wrong. That's what started us off, me and Rosamund. We'd bought some flashy notebooks, very large ones, because we'd tried to buy proper autograph books and couldn't get any.

'When we had an autograph, we used to write up afterwards on the next page how we felt, you know, whether we'd enjoyed meeting the person or if it was a show or something of the kind, whether we'd bother going to see them again. We even had a system for marking out of ten.' She shook her head at the recollection. 'We were so young and naive in those days. I know we progressed to writing down about what we thought of possible boyfriends, too.'

Jennifer felt the first stir of excitement. 'Did you throw the notebooks away in the end?'

'Do you know, I'm not sure. We used to swap them, read each other's, even add our own comments sometimes. Those notebooks ended up more like diaries or journals.' She sighed, shaking her head. 'Amazing, recalling memories, one seems to beget another like threading beads on a necklace.'

'Do you think you could have a look when you get time, Anya? See if you can come across it.'

'I will, certainly. But it must be at least five or six years ago, so I'm not that hopeful.'

'Well, not to worry if you've thrown it out.'

'Is it important?'

Jennifer spread out her hands. 'I

don't know. I'm trying to piece together Rosamund's earlier life. Mum and Dad aren't too happy about it. They're afraid it might cause problems. But I feel, for Ellie's sake, I at least have to try.'

'Do you know, it seems unbelievable, but I don't recall ever seeing Ellie. After we left school, Rosamund and I seemed to lose touch. She never called at the farm any more and before that she was quite a frequent visitor. And of course, I'd gone on to college to take a catering course. Still, I suppose having a baby to look after at such a young age is an enormous responsibility.'

'She seemed to cope fine, well, for the first couple of years whilst I was living at home. When Hal and I split up, of course, I took a job in Lambourn so the last year is pretty much blank.'

Outside a car door slammed and was followed seconds later by the kitchen door opening.

Anya looked up. 'That's Hal back, now.'

'I must go.' Jennifer sprang up and

replaced her cup on the tray. 'Thank's so much, Anya. You've been a real help. I feel I know much more now about Rosamund as she was at sixteen.'

'Please, Jennifer,' Anya put out a hand and caught her arm, 'please say you'll come again. I get so lonely for young company, you wouldn't believe. I was looking forward so much to you coming . . . ' Her voice choked and tears glinted on her lashes.

Unseen by either women, Hal had entered the room. He caught the last few words, the break in his sister's voice, saw the edge of tears.

'I don't want Anya upsetting, you know,' he said in a flat voice.

Both women swung round, startled.

'I thought your visit would be a happy one, cheer her up.' He frowned at Jennifer. 'Looks like I was wrong.'

Jennifer stifled the hurt she felt at his unjust words. 'Yes, Hal, you *are* wrong. If you think I would come as a guest and then upset her, you can't think too highly of me.'

'Oh, please . . . ' Anya looked from one to the other, unsure how to smooth the sudden friction but very aware of the undercurrent of other strong emotions.

'Don't worry, Anya.' Jennifer, feeling slighted as Hal continued to frown at her, picked up her car keys. 'And thanks again.' She headed for the door. 'I'll give you a call.'

8

Still feeling hurt and unsettled when she reached Swallow House, Jennifer parked the Mini and went straight to the stables to find some consoling peace. Always, when in need of comfort, she invariably found the horses provided it. Opening the bottom half of Dixie's stable door, she slipped inside.

But she wasn't alone. Peter was hunkered down in the straw beside Dixie. The horse was covered in sweat and obviously distressed. All thoughts of herself vanished as she stared down in dismay at her best-loved horse.

'Dad?'

'Thank the Lord you've come back, Jennifer.' He got up. 'Don't rightly know what's wrong with him, he could be just cast but I suspect it's colic.'

'How long has he been like it?'

'Can't have been long. He was certainly alright after lunch.'

'Have you rung the vet?'

'Yes, but that wasn't much help. Phillip's been called out to another emergency and his partner's away on holiday. I've left a message for Phillip to come straight over the moment he gets back.'

'In the meantime, it's up to us, yes?'

'Looks like it, me duck. We'd better try and get him up and walked, in case it is colic. Can you fetch his bridle and lead rein.'

'Right.' Jennifer did as her father instructed.

A fraught ten minutes followed whilst they struggled to alternatively encourage the horse to help himself and haul him up between them. They were both panting with exertion and as drenched in sweat as the horse when, with a mighty groan, Dixie heaved himself up onto his front legs and with a supreme effort, stood up shakily on all fours.

'Well done, Dixie.' Jennifer patted the

sweat-soaked neck encouragingly. 'Come on, old chap, let's get you outside and move you round a bit.' Peter leaned his weight against the horse's hindquarters whilst Jennifer took the leading rein and gently tugged him forward.

Once outside, it was easier to turn him in circles in the yard. But every now and then he would hesitate, swing his head round towards his belly and begin to sag.

'We'll just have to keep him going until Phillip gets here, but I'll see if I can find the drencher to give him a draught.'

Jennifer nodded, she needed all her strength to hold his head up and prevent him from going down. Horses were immensely strong, powerful creatures when compared to the strength of a man and, when in pain or frightened — and Dixie was both right now — were unpredictable. It was up to her to do all she could to help ease him.

Dixie gave a deep groan and swung

his head round suddenly, trying to bite at his soft underbelly. The leather rein Jennifer was holding was snatched smartly through her fingers, burning the skin. Catching her breath against the sudden pain, she took a firmer hold. It made her very aware of how puny and insignificant human beings were compared to horses.

'Steady now, boy, steady now,' she crooned to the big animal.

'You OK?'

'Sure.'

Peter shot her a sideways look before heading for the cottage. He was a believer in the power of giving love and the soothing touch. However, he knew Dixie was suffering great pain and was uncomprehendingly frightened. It was not a happy combination in a potentially dangerous animal.

Jennifer continued to croon soothing nonsense whilst at the same time she reached up to Dixie's ear and very tenderly stroked it from base to tip, pulling it gently downwards towards his temple. She deliberately poured out unconditional love, willing the big animal to accept it and feel the healing qualities that the love contained.

For several minutes she concentrated, and then with relief, felt the quivering flesh slowly begin to respond to the calming techniques. Dixie understood she was trying to help him. She knew he, like little Ellie had done, would be feeling all the comfort of caring love, soothing the pain, healing, relaxing the stress and tension. It would be calming and balancing his own body energy system.

She led him forward and did a wide circle of the stable yard. His trembling now had eased dramatically and he walked slowly, trustingly beside her, his eyes almost closed. Clearly whatever pain level he'd experienced, if not completely gone, was so moderated as to cause him much less discomfort now. 'Well done, boy,' Jennifer murmured, patting him. 'Just keep it going. You'll be fine once Phillip turns up.'

Together, they continued walking slowly, harmoniously, round and round the stable yard. For how long she had no idea, there was a mesmerising quality to walking in circles, but all the time she poured out unconditional love and the horse unresistingly accepted the healing.

Her lifelong association with horses, as well as dogs and other animals, had given her insights into their needs, emotional as well as physical. And she had long thought that the reason love was so successful at helping to heal with animals was because they did not throw up any mental barriers or negative doubts like most human beings.

Dixie blew gustily down his nostrils, leaning his head heavily against her. Jennifer stroked his neck, marvelling that he seemed to have actually stopped sweating. 'Well done, boy.'

Behind her, she heard a car drawing up and a door slamming. Moments later, the vet was striding across the yard towards her.

'Hello, Phillip.' He was only a few years older than herself but was a superb professional and a family friend of many years standing.

'Jennifer,' he smiled. 'What's his problem? Colic?'

'Hmm, I guess so. Although, he seems quite a bit better now.'

'Let's have a look at him.'

Dixie snorted, rolling his eyes with mistrust and swinging his hindquarters sideways, but Phillip deftly avoided the iron-shod hooves and ran experienced hands over the horse's belly.

Dixie flinched and lashed out with his hind legs as Phillip pressed on one particular area.

'Yes, I think you're right. We'll fix up a drench. Hopefully, he'll be OK fairly soon.'

'I have to confess, Phillip, I've given him a load of TLC. He certainly seemed to appreciate it.'

He cocked an eyebrow. 'And do you consider it's helped him?'

She gave him a brief smile. 'I *know* it has.'

Phillip was searching his bag for a specific instrument. He withdrew what looked like an enormous syringe. It was very familiar to Jennifer. 'He still needs a drench.'

'Yes, I know.'

'It should be easier to administer now he's quieter.'

'Well, I couldn't bear to see him suffer and tender loving care was about all I could do. That and try to keep his spirits up, of course.'

He winked at her. 'I won't tell if you won't.'

She laughed. 'Deal.'

'Let's get his head up now then and get this stuff down his neck.'

Jennifer was only too eager to assist. Her earlier efforts had relaxed the horse and, by so doing, had eased his pain and in short prepared him to accept the vet's very necessary professional help. It was a working partnership that benefited the patient.

Peter had come across the yard when he'd spotted the vet's vehicle. 'Thought we'd have to manage without you, Phillip.'

'Yes, difficult when there's only one of us on duty. However, the cow had managed to calve by the time I got to the farm. So, when I got the message on my mobile, I came straight here.'

'I appreciate your help. How's the horse doing?'

'He'll be fine. We've got the draught down him.' Phillip smiled. 'Your daughter's got the right touch, I must admit. He was in a pretty good receptive state when I arrived. Took it like a lamb having a bottle.'

'Still,' Peter clapped him on the shoulder, 'thanks again, Phillip.'

'No problem.' The vet swung his bag into the back of the Range Rover. 'Bye, then, I'm off. Sunday dinner is calling.'

* * *

By the time Jennifer followed Peter across to the cottage for their evening meal, she was feeling emotionally drained. It was surprising how much Hal's curtness had affected her. But the very fact that it had told her a great deal about her own feelings for him. And it also confirmed what she already knew, the farm and his family came first — that and the continuity of the family name. And she didn't want to be an also ran. The man she married, if she ever did, would have to give her his love unreservedly, put her first on his agenda.

Thinking about it, she became aware that what she wanted from Hal was something she herself wasn't prepared to do. The revelation really shook her. She was well aware that the people around you mirrored parts of yourself. Now she had just worked out Hal was showing her a part of herself she found unattractive and unacceptable. No doubt it would be called positive consciousness growth. However, it left her feeling confused and unsure how to deal with what the perception had shown her. Except that one thing was quite clear: if she didn't address this less than admirable trait in her own make-up, how on earth could she expect Hal to alter? The change had first to come within herself.

She placed a tired hand across her forehead. For now she would simply back off and allow herself to eat and rest, show herself the love she desperately needed. Acknowledging the lesson would be enough for the present. Life would unfold at it's own perfect pace, of that she was quite sure.

Kathleen had set the dining table and Ellie was already perched in her chair, a napkin tied around her neck. Seeing Jennifer, she crowed with delight and waved a colourful lidded beaker. 'Auntie Jen, Auntie Jen, I've drunked all my juice.'

'Have you, darling? Would you like some more?'

'Yes, yes.' She jiggled perilously in the chair.

Kathleen brought over a large roast of beef and placed it in the centre of the table. 'She's been a really good girl this afternoon.'

'I've been colouring pictures.'

'Lovely.' Jennifer set down the replenished orange juice. 'After our meal you can show me what you've done.'

Ellie smiled with satisfaction. 'What did you do, Auntie Jen?'

'Granddad and I were looking after Dixie because he was poorly.'

'How poorly?'

'He had a nasty pain in his tummy.'

Peter reached for the carving knife and fork and proceeded to meticulously cut off succulent slices of beef.

'Did you make it better, Auntie Jen?'

'The vet came to help us at the end.'

'Why not at the beginning?' Ellie wrinkled her nose in a frown.

'Because he was busy helping a cow to have a baby calf.'

'Oh.' She pondered on this.

'He came and made Dixie better on his way home.'

'This beef is a cow.' She pointed a rigid forefinger at the slice of meat Peter had just placed on her plate.

'Well, yes.'

Ellie's frown deepened. 'I'm not eating a cow, cows live in fields.'

'This one's not alive now,' Peter said.

The child's face crumpled. She pushed away her plate with both hands and tears began to trickle.

'Oh well done, Peter.'

'Never mind, Dad.' Jennifer leaned across and deftly swapped Ellie's plate for her own empty one. 'Tell you what, Ellie, how about I make some cheesy sauce and you can pour it all over your vegetables? You'd like that for your meal, wouldn't you?'

Fists pushed tight against her closed eyes, Ellie hesitantly nodded.

'Good girl.' Jennifer went to the fridge and took out cheese and milk. 'Why not choose your veggies, whilst I fix the sauce.'

Kathleen exchanged a look with Peter. 'Blessed are the peacemakers . . . '

He lifted the lids on the tureens. 'Here you go, little 'un, take your pick, orange, yellow and green: carrots, sweetcorn and peas.'

A watery smile crossed the child's face. 'You've forgotten the red, Granddad.'

'Eh?'

She pointed to a dish of beetroot. 'It's a rainbow.'

'So it is. Come on then, tuck in.'

With infinite care, Ellie arranged all the different colours to her satisfaction.

Jennifer poured the sauce into a spare gravy boat and set it down beside her. 'All yours.'

'Hmmmmm, nice.' Ellie liberally covered her plate and began to eat with rapt attention.

'I usually try and disguise the meat,' Kathleen murmured very quietly. 'It doesn't always work.'

'I really wouldn't bother. Far better not to make meals confrontational.' Jennifer helped herself from the tureens. 'Ellie seems to prefer a vegetarian diet.'

'Best to go along with it then.'

Jennifer smiled at her mother. 'As long as she's getting all the protein she needs for growth, cheese and fish, say, that's all that matters. It's important she enjoys her food.'

'Well, she does eat a lot of cheese, I'd noticed that a long time ago. Rosamund was a lot more easy going with her. She used to maintain the child knew best what suited her system. I think it's just me who finds her a bit of a handful.'

'I am sorry if you missed your afternoon nap with me going up to the farm.'

'Doesn't matter, I'll probably have an early night instead.'

'How did you get on, up the farm? Did you meet Hal?' Peter speared a piece of roast beef, took a deep appreciative sniff and cheerfully tucked in. 'This is really excellent beef.'

'I didn't go to see Hal, I went to see Anya.'

'Yes, well . . . I know that,' he

munched appreciatively, 'but you weren't serious, were you?'

Jennifer swallowed hard as the food stuck in her gullet. 'As it happens, Dad, yes, I was.'

'Oh.' He paused, fork half-way to his mouth. 'Whatever for?'

'Peter, don't you think you've put your foot in it enough this mealtime?' Kathleen said with a meaningful glance towards Ellie.

'What? Oh . . . right, I see.' He, too, glanced at the child but Ellie was in a world of her own.

'Red and yellow and pink and green, orange and purple and blue,' she was singing softly to herself as she spooned up the vegetables, 'I can sing a rainbow . . . '

'Bless her,' said Kathleen, 'she does love colours.'

Ellie stopped singing and looked up at her grandma. 'They're rainbow colours, Grandma.'

'Yes, darling, they are.'

'This one's green.' Ellie stabbed a

pea and held up her fork for Jennifer's inspection.

'That's right, darling.' Jennifer pointed to the carrots. 'What colour are those?'

'Orange,' the tot nodded firmly.

Peter, however, was still frowning. 'What did you mean?' he persisted. 'I don't know, really, you women . . . What on earth has Hal done that you don't want to see him? I mean, only the other day he was good enough to give you and little 'un a lift back to save you walking home in that storm.'

'Shush, Peter.' Kathleen cast an anxious glance at Jennifer.

Peter shook his head. 'I just don't get it. You shouldn't encourage her, Kathleen.'

'Pardon me!'

'Well, be rational, woman. Hal's a good bloke, sound. Everybody knows that.'

Desperate to get away from the subject of Hal, Jennifer said, 'Anya discussed Rosamund's friends with me.'

'Why?'

'Look, Dad, I didn't think it was

right to begin with, Rosamund not telling us who the man was. OK, yes, it was her business, but we are . . . ' she bit her lip, 'we were . . . her family. She certainly needed all the support that we could offer but now . . . '

Kathleen reached across the table and covered Jennifer's hand with her own. 'You don't have to go on, love.'

'But I do, Mum. It matters a great deal to me, and in the future it will matter a great deal to —' She inclined her head in Ellie's direction. The child, however, was happily oblivious to the grown-ups' conversation. 'If there's a chance of discovering who *he* is then I'm going to do all I can to find out. None of us knows what the future holds and it might just turn out that she will need someone else's support if we aren't around to give it.'

Both her parents were staring at her.

Finally, Kathleen said, 'Are you serious, Jennifer?'

'Yes, Mum, I'm deadly serious.'

Peter laid down his knife and fork.

'It's very upsetting, Jennifer.'

Jennifer, realising it was an emotive subject, said, 'Don't worry, Dad. I'll be very discreet.'

'You'll need to be.'

'I will, I promise!'

'If you say so.' He dropped the subject abruptly and applied himself to his meal.

'Pretty colours, Granddad,' Ellie piped up and gave him one of her mega-watts heart-melting smiles.

Despite his prickliness in the face of something he didn't approve of, he returned her smile. It was impossible not to. 'Whatever makes you happy, my little 'un.'

Jennifer sighed with relief. She would not have brought up the subject at dinner time but it was better to have it out in the open.

'Pudding, everyone?' Kathleen put in quietly, anxious to normalise and smooth over the delicate, uncertain atmosphere. 'It's fruit crumble.'

'With custard, Grandma?'

'Yes, darling, with custard.'

9

Standing in front of the old cottage door, Jennifer caught her breath. The knocker screwed to the door was a 'points-up' for luck horseshoe. At Swallow House they had a horseshoe knocker just like this one. She wondered why Maud had chosen it. Was it possible she also had a connection with horses? She grasped the knocker. It would be a wasted journey if Maud wasn't home.

It was nearly a week since she'd talked with Anya but the stable had had runners on three of the days and there simply hadn't been time to go trekking to the village. A quick scan of the telephone directory had proved abortive. Either she was ex-directory or, more likely, didn't possess a phone. In the end she'd had to resort to looking up Maud's address in the Register of Electors. She lifted the horseshoe and knocked twice — and waited.

There was a movement inside the cottage, a chair was scraped back against a bare stone floor. Jennifer heard a tapping sound and correctly deduced it was probably a white stick and allowed extra time for the old lady to reach the door.

What she would ask Maud was a mystery. It was the height of rudeness asking her to betray Rosamund's confidences, if indeed, she was party to them. But what other course was there? Briefly, Jennifer considered a swift retreat but even as she thought it, the door swung open and a tiny much-wrinkled old lady stood there.

'Who is it?' She angled her head seventy degrees in order to peer up at Jennifer's face.

'Hello, it's Maud, isn't it?'

'Yes.'

Jennifer took a fragile hand in hers. 'I'm Jennifer Dunbar. You remember Rosamund Dunbar? Well, I'm her elder sister.'

'Aaah . . . ' A sweet smile spread over her face. 'Come along in, I thought one day you'd come a-calling on me.'

'You did?' Jennifer followed Maud and her tapping stick through to the cosy, over-furnished sitting room.

'Near on like a daughter she was to me. A lovely girl, lovely, and now, she's gone, too. Eh, life's hard, me duck, ain't it?'

Jennifer feeling a lump rise in her throat nodded, then realising Maud couldn't see, said, 'It's no easy ride for sure.'

'Sit you down. There's a jug of lemonade over on the sideboard. Pour us both a drink, me duck.'

Pleased to have something to occupy her hands whilst she gained control of her emotions, Jennifer did so.

'I miss her coming.' Maud's mouth worked. 'Used to read to me, you know. She was grand company. Brought the babby as well, soon as she was born. Used to put her on the sofa,' she waved a hand to a chintzy covered monster along the far wall. 'Packed her round with cushions and gave her a rattle or a fluffy toy.

'Rosamund would make us a pot of tea and we'd maybe have a slice of cake or a biscuit. Then she'd read the next part of the book.' Maud sighed deeply. 'Of course, I thought I'd go before she did but you never know when your time's up. I'd made my will, y'see, making her a beneficiary.'

Jennifer's eyes widened in surprise. 'But Rosamund wouldn't have wanted or expected you to.'

'Tush . . . ' Maud fumbled for Jennifer's arm and patted it. 'I *know* that, 'course I do. I *wanted* to. She brought a lot of light into my life. I lost my own daughter when she was thirteen, caught meningitis, she did.'

'I'm sorry, I didn't know that. What a shock. Did your husband support you?'

Maud laughed softly. 'Eh, lass, your generation think you've invented sex. Let me tell you it was around a long, long time before you were born. No, I'd no husband, he was already married. Well, near as, he was engaged to someone else, y'see.'

'You sound as though you were better off without him.'

'Aye, an that's what I thought an' all, despite knowing him all my life.'

'Rosamund wasn't married, you did know that didn't you?'

'Oh aye. Reckon that's where our bond came from, shared experience, y'see.'

Jennifer felt a quickening of excitement. 'Do you want to tell me?'

'I kept quiet about who my babby's father was, well, it would have caused a right kerfuffle seeing as he was a family friend. It would have caused a lot of hurt all round. Best I kept it secret.'

'Rosamund said the same thing.'

'Aye, she was a lot like me, in my younger days.'

'Do you know who the father of Rosamund's baby is?'

'Yes.' Maud reached out sensitive, searching fingers and closed them around her glass of lemonade. She took a long drink. 'Yes, me duck, I know who he is.'

* * *

Jennifer went straight up to her room when she got back home. She was unlikely to doze off, there was no time. The evening shift in the stables began in a few minutes. She'd used nearly the whole of her afternoon break talking to Maud. Apart from that, her mind was racing with all the things Maud had told her.

Pulling off her outer clothes, she lay down on the bed and willed herself to relax. The old lady had refused to say who Ellie's father was. Jennifer had pressed her but she'd remained adamant. Jennifer knew it was a ploy. The old lady was lonely and she could sympathise but to be so close to finding out the man's name was more than frustrating.

'Come and see me again and I'll see

about telling you his name. Bring the toddler an' all. I'd dearly love to see her again.'

'I will, I promise.' Then she couldn't help adding, 'And not just to find out. Rosamund would want me to, I know.'

'Bless you, me duck. You are both a pair of good 'uns.'

Jennifer had embraced her. 'Thank you for all the support you gave Rosamund. I know it must have helped her.'

'I think it did,' she nodded. 'A lot of the time, though, she talked about you.'

Jennifer had been surprised. 'Why me?'

'She was concerned about you, and your future.'

'Really?'

'And I'm saying no more, not yet.' Maud had grinned roguishly.

Her words had left Jennifer more confused than ever. Rosamund had never hinted at any fears about her future.

Jennifer tossed restlessly in the single

bed. She had a horrid feeling she was not going to like knowing the answers. Maybe, after all, Rosamund had been right in stating it shouldn't be brought to light.

The telephone beside her head jangled into life making her piano-tight nerves jump. She snatched it up quickly before the noise could disturb everyone else. With three days racing already this week, it had meant Peter had missed a lot of his afternoon naps. In racing, with such early working starts, it was a given the afternoon nap was sacrosanct.

She held the phone to her ear. 'Swallow House Racing Stables.'

'Jenny, it's Hal. Please don't put the phone down.'

Even if her nerves weren't overstrung, her heart would have begun to beat faster. Just the sound of his voice made her insides melt. Taking several deep breaths to calm herself, she said, 'Hello, Hal, anything wrong?'

'No, nothing.' He hesitated. 'I need to see you, Jenny. Anya's put me square.

I'm sorry I jumped to conclusions. And I'm really sorry I upset you. Look, please, would you have dinner with me?'

'I . . . I'm not sure.' It was so unexpected Jennifer felt wrong-footed.

'Tomorrow, Saturday,' he rushed on, 'I'm afraid I can't invite you for Sunday dinner, we're expecting Anthony and his family up from London, but I know how busy you are. Please, Jenny, say you will.'

Suddenly she was tired, so very tired of pushing water uphill, fighting off her feelings of longing and love for this man. She remembered how comforting and right it had felt when they'd been coming back with Ellie in the Land Rover.

'Jenny, are you still there?'

'Pick me up at seven o'clock, Hal, OK?'

He released a long sigh, 'Bless you, Jenny, seven it is, Saturday.'

With a shaking hand she set the phone down and flopped back limply on the bed.

Down the far end of the landing she

heard her parents' bedroom door open and footsteps going down the staircase. She swung her legs out of bed, pulled on her working gear and trotted down to Ellie's door.

Popping her head round, she found herself gazing into two deep pools of blue as Ellie, just waking, held both arms high in the air to be lifted up. She bent over the child's bed, scooped her up and sat hugging her close, rocking them both. Whether she was soothing Ellie or herself was immaterial. It was an instinctive mothering gesture and Ellie was as near to being her own child as it was possible to get.

Jennifer squeezed her eyes tightly shut. Being sterile was a burden she was forced to carry. Now, thinking about it as she hugged the little girl close, unshed tears oozed from beneath her lashes. Was she mad? She'd just accepted a dinner date with Hal and it was a sure fire way of self-destructing.

Ellie squirmed on her lap. 'Go down, Auntie Jen.'

Jennifer blinked rapidly. 'Off you go then, my angel. We'll go and see Grandma in the kitchen. You'd like some juice wouldn't you?'

'Juice, juice, juice,' Ellie bounced up and down, re-energised after her afternoon nap. She headed downstairs at a fine lick. Jennifer followed rather more slowly.

Kathleen had just made a large pot of tea. 'Did I hear the phone?'

'Yes, it was Hal.'

'And what did he want?'

'To take me out to dinner tomorrow night.'

Kathleen swung round her eyes very wide. 'And?'

Jennifer swung Ellie up into her chair and collected a beaker of chilled apple juice from the fridge. 'There you go.'

Ellie clutched it with both hands. 'Thank you.'

'Good girl.'

'And?' repeated Kathleen.

'Oh, alright. I said yes.'

'Well, that's a relief.'

'What is?' Peter queried, coming into the kitchen. 'Ah, yes, tea.'

Kathleen and Jennifer looked at each other and smiled.

'Men!' Kathleen shook her head, 'Simple souls, aren't they, easily satisfied.'

'What have I said now?' Peter looked bewildered.

'Nothing, Dad, nothing at all. We were just saying Hal's phoned and I've said yes to dinner with him tomorrow night.'

He grunted. 'About time, too.'

* * *

'I think I'll take my coffee up and drink it in the bath. You don't mind, do you?' Jennifer had volunteered to make drinks for herself and Kathleen. They were relaxing after dinner watching a mediocre film on television. Peter was out at the pub.

Kathleen yawned widely and accepted the mug of scalding coffee. 'Not in the least. I should imagine you could do with some space.'

'It has been a people crowded day, yes.' What she didn't add was she yearned to be on her own to mull over all the intriguing things Maud had told her and also to consider what she felt about Hal's offer of a dinner date. It had been the easiest thing to agree when he was pushing her but she was questioning the wisdom of her acceptance.

Minutes later, lying soaking in the fragrant water, she ran through her conversation with Maud. Although Ellie's father's name had not been voiced, there were clues in what the old lady had said. It seemed Rosamund's situation had mirrored a lot of Maud's past. A family friend of many years, Maud had divulged. This would suggest she herself knew him. And he would seem to have been engaged to another woman.

Jennifer finished her coffee and lay back in the bath and closed her eyes.

Who fitted that scenario? It might be a good idea to check in the register of marriages for weddings that had taken place that year. She gave an impatient shake of her head. No, that wouldn't work. More than likely, the bride would hold the wedding in her own village. There didn't seem to be any logical way to check.

Obviously, it wasn't someone from her own extended family. So, what friends had married? Bill Burton, the farrier's son Jake, had but he wasn't exactly a friend, more a business acquaintance. Two of the lads in the yard had also tied the knot, they certainly were friends. And with Rosamund's looks she knew they had both carried torches for her sister.

Jennifer racked her brains. The vicar's son, Jeremy, had hastily married on the rebound when his former girlfriend had ditched the boy she'd been going out with. That had caused a stir in the village. Could it have been Jeremy? He'd been friendly with Rosamund.

Had he looked for consolation with her only to find his first love available again? And there was Phillip, of course. He was a lot older than Rosamund but training to be a vet had taken seven years. He'd been dating another girl for years, not married certainly, but having grown up together it had been understood they would. Imagine if any one of those men proved to be Ellie's father, what an uproar it would cause. Rosamund had foreseen the consequences.

Jennifer pressed her fingers against both temples. She was getting a headache. She began to see Kathleen's point in urging not to dig up the past. For now she decided, she would do as her mother wanted — let it go. If Maud ever decided to tell her, then she, Jennifer, would also take the decision whether or not to make it public.

Reaching forward, she turned on the tap and let hot water gush. She leaned back and slid lower in the now beautifully warm water. Her thoughts turned to Hal and his pleading for her to agree to meet him. She wondered where he intended to take her. Most certainly it wouldn't be the village pub. It would be like living in a glasshouse, on view to everyone, with speculation rife as to whether they'd made it up, and whether, in the end, they'd walk down the aisle. No, Hal would have more sense than that, so it would be somewhere far enough away to warrant taking her in his car.

And there was the inevitable question of what she would wear. Would Hal wear a suit? Her heart began to thump as she visualised him. Hal was an attractive man even dressed in working clothes but scrubbed-up and in a suit, he was a very handsome man. Definitely not something sexy then, she decided hastily. The circumstances between them were still unchanged, still unsurmountable whichever way you looked at them. And if, in the end, she couldn't face him she could always chicken out, give him a ring.

Guiltily, she suddenly remembered she'd promised to ring Anya. She stood up dripping water and bubbles and lifted her wristwatch from the window ledge. No, it was far too late tonight, it would have to be tomorrow now. Reaching for the big white bath towel, she wrapped it snugly around her. It was hardly worth getting dressed again. She put on a nightdress and dressing-gown.

She padded down the landing passed Ellie's room where the child was fast asleep and on to her own room. But, hand on the doorknob, she hesitated and looked further along the landing to the last door — Rosamund's room.

Anya's words came back to her. 'It was more like a diary, or journal rather than an autograph book.' Suppose, just suppose, Rosamund had kept the journal — and written down the man's name. She let her hand drop from the knob and walked slowly on down the landing.

The door wasn't locked. Closing it

quietly behind her, she leaned against it and fumbled in the dark for the light switch. Once illuminated, the room appeared welcoming. She could sense Rosamund's personality in the pink-fluted bedside lamp — pink had been her sister's favourite colour — the bookshelves set in the wall containing an eclectic choice of novels, classics as well as modern, the cosy sheepskin rug that positively invited you to curl your toes in it.

Jennifer stood still and let her gaze travel around the room drinking in the essence of her sister. It was the first time she'd set foot here since Rosamund's death. Obviously, her mother had left everything exactly as it had been. The room was clean; in fact, it was spotless, but nothing appeared moved or altered in any way.

Jennifer moved over to the dressing-table. Her sister's hand mirror, brush and comb still rested on the glass top. She picked up the silver-backed hair-brush. Caught within the bristles were several hairs. The poignancy hit her and she sat down quickly on the tapestry-covered stool. 'Oh, Rosamund,' she whispered out loud, 'if only we could turn back the last year and re-live it differently.' She stared dry-eyed into the mirror in front of her and the reflection stared back. For several minutes she simply sat there feeling a strong closeness to her sister.

Lifting her gaze she became aware of the reflection of the room behind her. The mirror was set at an angle and showed the opposite wall from a different perspective. She leaned forward a little bit and narrowed her eyes. There was something odd about the lowest shelf of the bookshelves. At one end the wood appeared thicker.

Jennifer swung round and looked at the shelf. From a normal viewpoint it appeared no different to the others. Getting up she went over and ran a hand at the back underneath the lowest shelf. Her fingers encountered a package affixed to the underside. The gap was narrow and she fetched the hand mirror from the dressing table and held it at the necessary angle. It showed up the underside of the shelf and the manilla envelope sellotaped to it. Piggling off the sticky tape, she was rewarded when the envelope dropped into her hands.

Sitting down before the mirror Jennifer took a deep breath and slit the flap open. A large mauve notebook with stiff covers fell onto her knee. Even before she opened it Jennifer knew it must be Rosamund's journal. This was what she had come searching for, the notebook she had hoped to find. If she hadn't sat down on the stool and stared into the mirror, she would never have thought of checking the back of that lowest shelf. The perfect hiding place, it was a sheer fluke that had delivered the notebook into her hands.

With shaking fingers she turned over the front cover and began reading.

And realised she had been wrong.

10

Deep disappointment flooded her. She stared down at the open page. The notebook wasn't Rosamund's journal after all. Reaction made her feel weak and shaky and the feelings were compounded as she realised the possible implications. This notebook had survived so it was equally possible that Rosamund's also might still be found. She closed the cover. She had no wish to pry and reading it was way off-limits.

This journal belonged to Anya.

Downstairs, the Grandfather clock chimed the hour. Suddenly, she felt very tired. Far from making her feel elated, finding Anya's journal had had the reverse effect. With an effort she rose to her feet, opened the top drawer of the dressing-table and slid the notebook out of sight.

Going down to the kitchen she made

a cup of camomile tea to soothe her inflamed nerves. Searching for some comfort food in the biscuit barrel brought Sandy from his basket to lean expectantly against her legs. Absently, she fondled the soft ears and rewarded his faithfulness with a piece of biscuit. She nibbled one herself and sipped the scalding tea. Just what was she going to do about Rosamund's journal?

A talk with Anya was the first step. But if Anya did manage to find it, she would obviously read it. And if she did, the name of Ellie's father might very well be written in it. Jennifer realised with a jolt she wanted to uphold Rosamund's wishes. It was far too personal and should not be made common knowledge. But as things stood it looked like she was not going to be able to honour her sister's wishes.

Beside her leg Sandy stiffened and gave one warning growl. Jennifer drew her dressing-gown closer and glanced towards the door. Seconds later Peter opened it.

'Oh,' she sighed, 'for a second there I wondered who it was.'

'Are you OK? You seem a bit jumpy.'

'Yes, sure.'

His face creased with concern. 'You look very pale.'

'I'm fine, Dad, really, just tired. I'm off to bed now. We've got runners tomorrow.'

'And you're going out for dinner, too, don't forget that.' He grinned. 'You'd better get some rest or you'll end up falling asleep in your soup.'

She bit her lip. Right now she'd give a lot not to be seeing Hal tomorrow. It could prove extremely awkward if she had any sort of emotional tussle with Anya over Rosamund's journal.

⋆ ⋆ ⋆

The next morning she'd ridden out first lot, gone in for breakfast and was down in the stable again grooming Dixie's shining coat. Holding his tail out she let part of it fall like a curtain as she made sure it was tangle-free and had no bedding caught in it. The Dandy brush swished through the long hairs bringing the tail to a cascade of perfection.

'You look a champion,' she told the big horse as he swung his head round and watched her. Fetching a bag of elastic bands, she moved close to his neck and began the time-consuming job of separating his springy mane into eleven equal sized plaits and securing them with the bands. She was about half-way down his neck when Dixie threw up his head and gave a whicker of recognition. 'Whoa, boy, steady, what is it?'

Jennifer turned as Kathleen and Ellie came into the stable. The child rushed up to Jennifer and clutched her tightly burying her face against her legs.

'Me too, me too,' she wailed.

'Whoa,' Jennifer picked her up and gently smoothed a finger across the wet cheeks brushing away teardrops.

'I'm sorry, Jennifer,' Kathleen shook her head, 'I can't deflect her.'

'Want to go to the races,' Ellie lifted a tear streaked face, 'want to come with you.'

'Well, little girls who cry can't go, that's for sure. They'd frighten the horses.'

Ellie snuffled and hiccuped into silence. 'Not crying, Auntie Jen.'

'Good girl.' Jennifer kissed her. She turned to Kathleen. 'We're at Nottingham so it's not far. How about you coming along as well, Mum? You could drive the car and follow the horse-box, couldn't you? We could stop at Colwick, say, drop Ellie off so you could bring her into the racecourse and then watch the parades and the races. What do you think?'

Kathleen looked from one to the other. 'Something tells me I don't have much choice.' But she was smiling. 'Why not, then. After all, next Saturday is your big race at Newmarket. There's no way we'll miss *that*.'

Jennifer's stomach knotted. Her father had been discussing this with her for the past two weeks. She had agreed to the ride, against her better judgement, because financially it was in the interests of Swallow House Stables. Not only was the race an extremely important one, but it also held enormous emotional impact. Last year she had ridden Dixie in this same race — and won — but it had cost her dearly. Putting the race first, before Hal, had cost them their relationship.

'Don't remind me, please, Mum,' Jennifer rolled her eyes. 'I'm trying not to think about it.'

'You won it last year. Let's see if you can make it a double.'

'Yes, I won,' she said quietly, 'but look what I lost — Hal.'

'Well, seeing that you're having dinner with him tonight, I don't go along with that.'

'I wish I hadn't agreed to. Please don't go getting your hopes up. I tell you, it's going nowhere.'

'OK, OK.' Kathleen lifted a placating hand.

'But this afternoon, we'll give Ellie a treat and take her to Nottingham races.'

* * *

At ten to seven that evening the telephone rang. It was Hal.

'Just thought I'd see if everything is still on for tonight. I didn't want to turn up if you'd changed your mind,'

Jennifer gripped the receiver. 'Yes, yes, dinner is still on.'

'Wonderful.' His voice glowed with pleasure. 'I wouldn't want to railroad you into coming if you really didn't want to.'

Jennifer gulped. He was giving her the chance to back out gracefully. Not many men would do that. 'No,' she said firmly, 'I'm all dressed-up and ready to go.'

'See you in ten minutes,' he said softly.

* * *

Seated in the passenger seat, Jennifer stretched out her legs in comfort as the powerful vehicle ate up the mileage down the country lanes. Emphasising his respect for her, Hal had left the Land Rover behind at the farm and instead had collected her in his Mazda sports car. Black, sleek and with the sun-roof down, it was impressive. But not as much as the man, himself.

Hal wore a navy blue suit and dazzling white shirt, open at the neck with a set of gold cuff links at the wrists. He smelt very nice, too, reminiscent of cedars and salt-spray.

'You don't look so bad, yourself,' he replied as she complimented him on his turnout. 'I've been working with the cattle this afternoon and I think I must have spent nearly an hour in the bath trying to get rid of the smell.'

She laughed. 'You certainly don't smell of cattle. Whatever the aftershave is, it was worth buying.'

He glanced quickly across at her and grinned. 'Your perfume should have a red alert warning especially when you wear it with that delight of a dress.'

'Thanks.' She felt the colour rise in her cheeks. She'd put on a light spray of Jessica McClintock 'White Flowers' perfume and eventually decided on a white cotton broderie Anglaise dress with a boat-shaped neckline. It was cool, unfussy and made her feel she wasn't giving off too many seductive vibes. But even from that swift glance, she'd seen the appreciative twinkle in his eyes and was wondering if jeans wouldn't have proved a safer choice.

Hal bent forward and switched on the CD player to allow Mozart to trickle through the speakers, filling the car with exquisite melody. Jennifer sighed with pleasure.

'Where are you taking me?'

'Trust me, you'll like it.'

She rested her head back and gave herself up to enjoying the lovely countryside of the vale of Belvoir, the tiny pretty villages and the rolling backdrop of densely wooded hills that seemed to stretch for miles. It held an enduring quality of stillness and permanence. In the gentle early evening sunshine, the English countryside was breathtakingly beautiful.

And on top of the skyline to the left was the famous Belvoir Castle, surveying the spreading vale below it with an almost benevolent air.

'Ireland is supposed to have forty shades of green, but just look at all that green splendour . . . ' she sighed with contentment. 'It's utterly glorious. Doesn't it make you so proud to be English, Hal?'

He glanced at her. 'I'm so pleased you feel like that, too, Jenny. This is my country, our country. I can understand how our young men felt who were called up during the war. I'd be prepared to die for it, too.' He slowed down to a crawl to allow her more time to drink it in.

'I don't want to think about death, Hal.'

Instantly, he put both feet down and

stopped the car. 'Darling Jenny, forgive me.' Before she knew what was happening, he'd gathered her into his arms and was tenderly kissing her forehead, cheeks, hair. 'I'm so sorry.' He held her close. 'I'm an insensitive fool.'

'Nothing to forgive,' she gulped, shaken by the way her body was responding to his caresses. 'I wasn't thinking of Rosamund . . . well, not at that moment. It's just the beauty of it all . . . ' She pulled away a little, trying to calm the racing of her heart.

Reluctantly, he released her. 'I would never intentionally hurt you, Jenny. I love you.'

Their faces were inches apart and the chemistry between them was electric.

Jennifer took a deep breath. 'Please, Hal . . . don't pressure me. I think we should drive on.' She gave a nervous little laugh. 'I always thought clinches came after dinner, not before.'

'Quite right, m'dam.' He slid in first gear and pulled smoothly away. Raising an eyebrow rakishly, he added, 'I'll remind you of that later.'

They motored on to Woolsthorpe and turned left at the base of the hill on which the castle stood. Now she could guess where he was taking her. But not for the world would she spoil his surprise. Only a short way farther on he turned sharp right off the narrow country lane on down a short entrance drive. It culminated in a wide car park, bounded on the eastern side by the Grantham canal, and parked in front of the entrance to the famous country pub, 'The Dirty Duck'.

He twisted in his seat. 'You knew, didn't you?'

'Well, I could lie . . . ' she began, smiling, 'but considering this is just about the best pub for food around here for miles, it wasn't hard.'

'And not considering we got engaged here,' he said lightly, watching her face.

'True.'

There was a moment of charged silence before he said, 'Well, what are we waiting for?' And he led her inside.

The pub was packed. The atmosphere of friendly cheerfulness was almost tangible.

'Good job I booked us a table.' He led her to one under the window beside the massive brick fireplace. He went to the bar, ordered their meal and returned to offer her a glass of white wine.

'Was it true the Duke of Rutland actually came in here for a drink?'

'I rather think it was. Course, its official name is 'The Rutland Arms' but everyone knows it as 'The Dirty Duck'.'

'Could have something to do with all the ducks swimming past on the cut.'

'Probably. Let's face it, the cut's only a few feet away — and the canal walk . . .' he buried his face in his glass of lager.

She took a sip of her wine. He didn't expect an answer and she didn't finish his sentence by saying, 'where you asked me to marry you.'

There was no point reliving the past.

The future was the thing.

'I do love the brasses all over the walls. I've never seen so many in a pub before. Look how they gleam, must take hours polishing them all.'

'Yes, it's certainly got character in spades.' Their meal arrived.

They ate in appreciative silence — the fish was truly excellent.

'What about a pudding?' Hal asked.

'Better not. I've got to watch my weight; only just scraped through this afternoon, and it's the big race coming up next week.'

'How did you do, today?'

She sipped some more wine. 'Dixie won.'

'You're too modest, Miss Dunbar.'

'It's my job, Hal.'

'I know.' He looked down at the table, repositioning his knife and fork. 'Jenny, I've been so stupid. I never realised what racing meant to you, does mean to you, not at the time it mattered. I know what I've thrown away and God help me, I beat myself up every day for letting my chance go.'

She reached out and covered his hand with her own. 'Don't do that to yourself, Hal. You're a good man. It was never your intention to deliberately hurt me — '

'And I wouldn't! Ever!'

'I know that, but I also know the farm and its future means as much to you as racing does to me.' He was silent, knowing the truth of her words. 'Anyway,' Jennifer sought to smooth the conversation, 'how are things at the farm?'

'Busy, a dawn-to-dusk job at the moment. You know, getting in the harvest.'

'Yes. Any chance you could watch me racing next Saturday?'

He looked at her steadily. 'No chance. Last year I lost most of the harvest.'

Jennifer started at him. 'Are you still blaming me for that?'

He shrugged and drained the last of his lager.

'Hal,' she clenched her fists beneath the table, 'I asked you a question.'

'Do you want the truth? I don't do lies.'

Her heart hammered uncomfortably. 'I'd like an honest answer, yes.'

With great deliberance, avoiding her eyes, he set the empty glass down on the table. 'Ask yourself whose fault it was. I think you'll find it was yours.'

She felt as though the floor had tilted beneath her. She took a deep, ragged breath hardly able to believe how the lovely evening had suddenly gone downhill. 'In that case, I'll make darn sure I don't get the blame this year.' She stood up on less than steady legs. 'I'd like to go home, please.'

* * *

'You must have gulped down your dinner,' Kathleen said in surprise as Jennifer walked in.

'Oh, the dinner was enjoyable, too bad the company didn't match it.'

Kathleen frowned. 'Do you want to tell me?'

'Not really.' Jennifer poured herself a glass of water. 'Sorry, Mum, but I did warn you not to get your hopes up. Seems I was right.'

'I'm sorry, love.'

'Well, at least I know where I stand. Anyway,' Jennifer bent and gave her mother a kiss, 'I'm straight to bed. See you in the morning.'

She ran upstairs. Taking off the white dress, she hung it back in the wardrobe. For a short time that evening, she had begun to think that there might be a chance for them. She had done what she'd warned her mother not to — raised her hopes. Then, emotion taking over, she threw herself down onto the bed and sobbed for what wasn't going to happen.

11

On Monday evening she rang Anya.

'Hello, Jennifer. Lovely to hear from you.'

'I thought about ringing yesterday but I knew Anthony and his wife were visiting.'

'It wouldn't have mattered,' Anya sighed, 'they couldn't make it.'

'Oh, bad luck.'

'To make it worse, Hal was in a filthy temper all day. He came home like it on Saturday night.'

'I'm afraid that was because we had words.'

'I told him off after you'd been to the farm. He got hold of it quite the wrong way round, silly man. Anyway, I told him he should apologise to you.'

'Yes, he did, thanks.'

'But things are still not right between you?'

'Afraid not.' Jennifer said it with a note of finality in her voice and Anya took the hint and didn't pursue it.

'I went to see Maud a few days ago.'

'How is she?'

'Well, I think. But she does miss Rosamund's visits. She's asked me to go again and to take Ellie as well. Apparently, Rosamund took Ellie with her when she went to read to Maud. It seems they share a similar back history.'

'Really?'

'Hmmm. Talking of reading, I've found a journal. To begin with I thought it must be Rosamund's but I opened it and realised straight away it's yours.'

'Oh, wonderful. Does it have a mauve cover?'

'Yes.'

'Well, Rosamund's was pink so it's definitely mine.'

'I didn't read it,' Jennifer assured her.

'Thanks, I appreciate that.'

'Do you think you could have a look for the pink one?'

'I will, yes, I'll have a good hunt round.'

'And if you do find it, Anya, could I ask you don't read it, please.'

'I certainly won't.'

Jennifer felt a great rock had rolled off her shoulders. 'Thank you so much.'

'Could I ask a favour?'

'Go ahead.'

'You say you're going to take Ellie to visit Maud. May I come, too?'

'Of course you can. I'm sure Maud would be delighted, she's very lonely. I was actually thinking of going on Wednesday afternoon because we don't have runners this week. Well, except for the Newmarket meeting on Saturday.'

'That's your big race isn't it?'

'It is.'

'Are you looking forward to it, or are your knees knocking?'

Jennifer laughed. 'I wouldn't be much use if they were. I need them to grip.'

'So you do,' Anya laughed, too. 'I could make Wednesday if you want to.'

'OK, we'll make it definite and I'll pick you up at the farm on the way — two o'clock suit you?'

'Lovely. I'll look forward to it.'

It wasn't until she'd put the phone down that Jennifer realised Maud had half-promised to reveal the name of Ellie's father. If she did, Anya would find out, too.

But having promised to take the girl — it was too late now.

* * *

'Which one would you like to wear, Ellie?' Jennifer had taken three little dresses from the wardrobe and laid them on the bed. 'We're going to see Maud. You don't know her but she knows you.'

Ellie tugged off her elastic-waisted trousers and, forefinger in her mouth, studied all three. 'Me choose, Auntie Jen?'

'Yes, darling, whichever you like.'

Jennifer hid a smile as the child, head on one side, solemnly deliberated the merits of each dress. Finally, taking the finger from her mouth, she pointed to a bright yellow dress. 'That one.'

'Sure?'

Ellie nodded vigorously and dragged off her T-shirt.

'Come on then, let's rig you up.' She slipped the crisp cotton dress over Ellie's head and secured the buttons.

'Take Loppy-lugs?'

'I'm sure Maud would like to see him.'

They went downstairs and Ellie dived on the furry toy where it lay in the pushchair.

'We're just off, Mum.'

Kathleen came through to the kitchen. Anxiety showed in her drawn face. 'I don't know whether to wish you good luck or hope she doesn't tell you.'

'I promised Anya I'd pick her up on the way, so it's too late now.'

'I know,' Kathleen sighed heavily. 'Whatever happens, happens.'

'Assuming I do find out who he is, would you rather I didn't tell you?'

'Let's wait and see how it goes.'

'OK.'

A couple of minutes later, with Ellie strapped into her car seat, Jennifer drove the Mini out of the gates and headed for Brackendown Farm.

Anya was all ready and waiting. She opened the passenger door and climbed in. 'Hello. You must be Ellie.'

'Ellie, this lady's name's Anya.'

The tot beamed up at her and held out the furry toy. ''S my rabbit.'

'Is it really? My, he's got long ears.'

'He goes to bed with me an' he has them underneath.'

Anya turned an enquiring look at Jennifer.

'She means Loppy-lugs has his ears tucked underneath the covers to keep him warm.'

'Oh right,' Anya nodded, 'good idea.'

Jennifer selected first gear and they were off.

'I've had a good look round but I'm sorry I haven't come across Rosamund's journal.' Anya grimaced. 'I really can't think where it could be lurking.'

Jennifer felt a stab of disappointment. She had been looking forward to reading it. It wasn't so much to find out if the man's name was written down but more to simply read her sister's thoughts, maybe her dreams, and to feel closer to her. 'It may still turn up. You could try asking your subconscious just before you go to sleep at night and see whether you have an idea next morning when you wake.'

'Would it work?' Anya sounded doubtful.

'I'm not saying it will, but it may very well do. I know I've tried it over the years on different subjects and been amazed at the results.'

'Oh well, in that case, I'll give it a go.'

Jennifer smiled. 'Keep an open mind and anticipate a result, it helps.'

'OK. I will.'

By now they'd reached the main street of the village and Jennifer pulled into the kerb beside a row of old cottages. She released Ellie from her seat, locked the Mini and together they walked up to Maud's front door.

When Maud opened it, she angled her head to try to see who it was. Ellie immediately angled hers so that she could look up into the old lady's face. Jennifer picked the child up. 'It's Jennifer, Maud and I've brought Anya Taylor and Ellie to see you.'

A beatific smile spread over the old lady's face. She put out a hand gently tracing the curve of the child's cheek. 'You've come a-calling again.' She waved them inside. 'Now, let me look at the babby. Put her down on the settee.' The old lady sat down beside her and Ellie beamed up at her. 'My, she's grown and just look at all her lovely curls.' She put out a thin hand and stroked Ellie's hair. She smiled at Anya. 'And thank you for coming as well, 'tis kind of you.' Turning to Jennifer, she said, 'Would you be Mother, me duck, and make us all a nice cup of tea? You'll find all the makings in the kitchen and there's a jug o' lemonade in fridge for this little 'un.'

'My Granddad calls me that,' Ellie said, nodding.

'Does he now?'

'Yes. And you're like Popeye.'

'Ellie!' Jennifer on her way to the kitchen swung round, scandalised. 'Say you're sorry, at once.'

' 'S true, Auntie Jen.' The child took one of Maud's fragile hands in hers and held it gently against her cheek.

'D'you mean, like Popeye and Olive Oil, in the films?' Maud queried.

Bewildered, the child shook her head. 'Popeye the horse. He's got poor eyes, too.'

Maud gave a chuckle. 'You're sharp as a tack, me duck.'

Ellie lifted Maud's hand to her lips and kissed it. 'Poor eyes,' she murmured.

Maud put an arm around her shoulders and hugged the child close. She waved Jennifer away in the direction of the kitchen. 'Off you go, we're getting on just fine, us two.'

Jennifer sighed with relief. For a

second there, she had regretted bringing the tot. Now, looking at them sitting close together on the settee, she could see the caring sensitive qualities Ellie possessed healing and uplifting the old lady. Young children were known to have a special empathy with the elderly and Ellie was clearly demonstrating this gift.

'Let me help.' Anya followed. She'd baked some individual cherry cakes and brought them to share.

They met with approval. Maud ate one and reached for a second. 'Any more tea in the pot?' she asked and Jennifer poured her a refill. The old lady sipped with enjoyment. 'By, it's nice having a bit of company.'

'Are we company?' Ellie asked, finishing her lemonade.

'You surely are.' She finished her cake and complimented Anya on being a good cook.

'I did intend to go into catering but with how things are, I can't.'

'Great pity about your Mam.' Maud

pursed her lips. 'Did for her, didn't it, losing your dad?'

Anya nodded. 'Yes, I'm afraid that's what started her depression.'

'Nay, lass, t'wasn't only that.'

Jennifer and Anya looked at each other in surprise.

'What do you mean? My mother was fine up until then.'

Maud put down her teacup and turned to Jennifer. 'You wanted to know about her dad,' she nodded towards Ellie. 'Well, it seems the right time to tell you, seeing as you're all here. This little 'un is Anthony Taylor's babby. And him engaged to another girl. That's what also upset Anya's mother.'

Jennifer didn't know how Anya was taking the news but she felt she had been double-barrelled by one of the horses — straight in her solar plexus.

* * *

Ellie's father was Hal's brother! For a moment everything receded and a roaring sound filled her ears. Desperately gulping air, she tried not to faint.

She bent her head forward and the roaring eased away to be replaced by a surge of indignation and anger. She spun round to face Anya. 'It was your brother.'

Anya had been sitting frozen with face devoid of all colour. Now, her face turned bright red. 'No, no, it wasn't. How dare you say such a thing, Maud. It wasn't Anthony, it wasn't, it wasn't.' Her voice had risen to screaming pitch and Ellie began to cry.

'I'm sorry 'tis such a shock for you but, as God's my witness, that's what Rosamund told me.'

Anya jumped to her feet. 'You're wrong. Anthony would never do such a thing.' She stumbled to the door.

Jennifer moved towards her but Maud put a hand on her arm, 'Let her be, it's the shock.'

Wrenching the door open, Anya slammed out.

Ellie, eyes big with shock and flooded

with tears clutched Jennifer. 'It's alright, darling,' she held the child close, soothing them both. Reaction was setting in and she was shaking.

'Seems I've upset all three of you. Well, it wasn't my intent an' p'raps I shouldn't have told you.' Maud's mouth worked.

'No, Maud, it isn't your fault. You were only passing on what Rosamund told you. But, oh dear, I see now why Rosamund wanted to keep it a secret. And why she was worried about how my future with Hal would be affected. Lots of people will be affected. Our lives are never going to be the same again.'

12

Jennifer's fingers felt stiff and clumsy. It had taken her twice as long as normal to put on the pink and blue racing silks. Most of the other jockeys were already streaming out from the changing room in a kaleidoscope of colour headed for the parade ring. She snatched up her crash cap and hastened after them.

The sultry hot air outside wrapped itself around her like a clinging blanket. The day would most likely end in a storm. She was reminded of this race, this time last year. If only there hadn't been a storm, she and Hal would still be together. Getting the ride had meant so much to her.

'Come and cheer me on, Hal,' she'd begged him.

'Sorry, Jenny, much too busy. I've still got a major part of the harvest to bring in.'

'This is the biggest race of my career.'

'But the weather's about to break and I want to get it all in.'

'So, what's more important to you, the farm — or me?'

Both under pressure, they knew this to be a test of commitment. 'Please, Hal. I so want you to be there.'

For a long moment he'd hesitated, face mirroring the turmoil going on inside. Then he'd groaned, clasped her face in both his hands and kissed her fiercely. 'You're the most important thing in my life, Jenny you always will be.'

And so he'd been there to cheer her on, to see her win the Newmarket Harlequin Stakes and nobody had been prouder.

Until they were on their way home up the A1. She'd left Joe to see to Dixie whilst Mike drove the horse box and opted to travel back with Hal in his car.

The day had been magical until ten miles from home when the first penny piece raindrops had begun to spatter across the windscreen. She'd seen his hands tighten on the wheel, knuckles turn white, seen his jaw clench rigidly and knew what they would find when they reached the farm.

The wheat crop, dry, golden nutrition, waiting to be harvested had been thrashed to the ground in great swathes by the force of the torrential thunderstorm. It was totally beyond saving.

It was the one and only time ever that Jennifer had seen Hal lose his temper — and it was spectacular.

'This is your fault, all your fault,' he'd raged. 'Begging me to go to Newmarket when I should have been here. The crop's ruined, all down the pan, and my income with it.'

She'd flung out of the car and gone home to Swallow House on foot.

The bell clanged and Jennifer's wandering attention snapped back to the parade ring as the announcer's voice called out 'Jockeys please mount'.

'No instructions, me duck.' Peter

cupped his hands and legged her up into the minuscule saddle. 'You know the horse inside out. Just come out of the stalls and win!'

'Do my best.'

'You'd better,' Peter grinned. 'Apart from Ellie and your mum, Hal's here now as well.' He pointed to a tall man threading his way urgently through the throng.

Jennifer's heart leapt. He'd put her first — left the harvest and the farm. Hal was here on her big day. Seconds later, a broad smile on his face, he'd cleared the crowd and was waving by the rail. Jennifer felt an uprush of love and exhilaration fill her.

The horses were starting to parade for the last time and as she rode past she just caught his words.

'Make it a double, Jenny. You and Dixie can do it.'

Raising a fist in the air in recognition, she followed the horses and jockeys out onto the racecourse.

It was a six furlong race and as the

stalls opened, the twelve horses catapulted forward. The pace was a fast one. Closely packed, the jockeys' colours were a bright sea above the sun-baked turf. Bending low over Dixie's neck, she watched the thrusting rumps of the three horses in front. The familiar sound of metal-shod pounding pistons hitting the ground at upwards of thirty miles an hour filled her ears. Dixie was making up ground and she eased him round on the outside and passed two of the leading horses.

With two furlongs left, the crowd watching from the stands roared their encouragement. Flicking the reins forward, Jennifer booted for home. The big horse responded instantly and came upsides with Seabird. They were racing neck and neck now, Seabird's jockey using the whip to urge on his horse, desperate to hold off Dixie's challenge. With yards left to go, racing nip and tuck and the crowd screaming hysterically, Jennifer worked hands and heels and asked Dixie for one last effort. The horses were racing head to head when Dixie stretched for home. He went a short head in front.

And the winning post came up and flashed by. They had made it!

* * *

There were celebrations at Swallow House Stables that evening. Kathleen beamed at her family and raised her glass of white wine. 'Congratulations, Jennifer, two on the trot.'

Jennifer inclined her head. 'And do I hear the echo of, 'let's make it a treble next year'?' They all laughed. Her win seemed to have brought them luck in the form of an email from Mr Redfern saying he'd watched the race on television and would be happy to have his horses stabled with Peter from the following week. Peter himself had been grinning from ear to ear ever since Dixie had won.

Jennifer looked at her parents with love. It was so nice to be able to give back something after all their years of hard work bringing her up. It didn't change anything regarding their combined loss of Rosamund but she could see the necessary healing was beginning. The only person missing tonight was Hal. He'd swept her up off her feet after the presentation of awards at Newmarket, and declared his love for her publicly. Then he'd said there was something he must do, kissed her and rushed away.

The telephone rang. Kathleen put down her wine and answered it. She held up the receiver. 'For you. It's Hal.'

Feeling the colour rush to her face, Jennifer said, 'I'll take it on the upstairs phone.' And dashed up to her room. Closing the door behind her, she lifted the receiver.

'That you, Jenny?'

'Yes, Hal, we're all partying. Like to come and join us?' She heard him laughing.

'I'd love to but at the moment I'm sitting in the Combine halfway across the thirty acre field.'

She gasped. 'You haven't finished the harvest? But you came to see me race.'

'Yes. I realised what a sap I've been. I was in danger of throwing you away — again! So, the crop has had to wait. However, I'm beavering away with all lights blazing.'

'I don't know what to say . . . ' Jennifer was filled with emotion.

'Say yes to coming over to the farm with Ellie for dinner tomorrow.'

Jennifer's thoughts spun to the last time she'd seen Anya. 'Oh, Hal, I don't think Anya would like me to.'

'Dear girl, Anya's the one who prompted me. She wants you here.'

Seizing the chance to make peace, Jennifer said, 'Then of course I'll come. Eleven-thirty OK?'

* * *

The storm broke at eleven-thirty on Sunday morning.

'Jennifer, Ellie, come in, quickly,'

Anya almost tugged them from the doorstep into the farmhouse. She closed the door and a tremendous squall of rain battered against it.

Jennifer shivered suddenly. 'Did Hal finish getting in the harvest?' It was the first question in her mind.

'Yes, thank heavens. He's in the sitting room with Mum. And before you ask the second question, Jennifer, no, I haven't told him about . . . Anthony.' She smiled down at Ellie.

'I assumed you hadn't. I haven't told my parents either, yet.'

'I didn't believe Maud,' Anya admitted, 'not then.'

'But you do now?'

'I did what you suggested and planted the question of where the pink notebook was in my mind before I went to sleep.'

'And?'

'I found it next day in an old handbag I was going to take round to give back to Rosamund and obviously never did.'

'So may I have it instead of this one?' Jennifer fished in her bag and drew out the mauve notebook.

'Of course, except . . . I have read it. Oh, I know I promised I wouldn't, but I needed to know for sure, either way.'

'What did it say?'

'Rosamund confirmed she was in love with Anthony.' For a second they simply stared before wrapping arms around each other and hugging tightly, both very near to tears.

'You'll have to tell Hal,' Jennifer gulped.

'Tell Hal what?' He came into the kitchen, swooped Ellie up into his arms and looked enquiringly at them.

'That Ellie's father is . . . our brother, Anthony.'

'Good God!' Hal sat down suddenly on a kitchen chair, the child still in his arms. He was silent, thinking back into the past. 'Yes,' he said slowly, nodding, 'it does explain things.'

Anya frowned, 'What things?'

'Like why they were together on two

or three occasions when I came across them . . . in our barn.'

Jennifer felt her legs go weak and sat down at the kitchen table. 'In our barn,' she repeated, the words now bringing up double images.

'What about Mother? Haven't you told her, Anya?'

'I think she already knows, Hal, has done from the beginning.'

'And that wouldn't have helped, would it?' He looked across at his sister.

'No.'

'But this little girl, being Anthony's child, might.' So saying, Hal lifted Ellie from his lap and took her through to the sitting room to meet Mary Taylor.

* * *

The storm lasted three hours, all the way through dinner. Hal had introduced her to his mother before dinner and seated them together. Jennifer looked up from her delicious meal, saw the wild storm-wracked sky from the window, and gave up a prayer of thanks that it hadn't come yesterday. Hal's arrival at the racecourse had spoken volumes. His love was all hers, she knew that now and her heart soared. But there was still one fact that could not be overlooked.

The meal had been superbly cooked and included a little vegetarian option especially for Ellie. The child was sitting next to Mrs Taylor chattering brightly and eating all before her. Jennifer smiled at Mrs Taylor and Mary smiled back. What a blessing the child was.

'That was a beautiful meal,' Jennifer said as she and Anya cleared the dishes from the table afterwards. 'I think you could make a success of a home-based catering business. That way you could still be here at the farm but be doing your own thing at the same time.'

'Never thought about that before, but I certainly will now, thanks.'

Jennifer reached for an apron to help with washing-up.

Anya waved a dismissive hand. 'No way.'

'Absolutely,' Hal seconded and took her arm. 'Look out there.' He pushed open the kitchen door. The world seemed washed and newly minted, the sun had come out and all the raindrops sparkled like jewels. 'Come on, we're going for a little walk.'

'Me too, me too.' Ellie was beside them in an instant.

'Do you mind, Hal?'

'Not if you don't.'

The three of them wandered out to look at the surrounding fields making up the farmland. Ellie, rejoicing in her freedom, scampered around happily.

Hal slipped his arm around Jennifer's waist. 'I want to ask you a question.'

'Before we go any further, Hal, I must tell you something first.' She couldn't leave him unaware of the harsh facts any longer. He needed to know. Her mouth felt dry, she had no idea how he would take the bad news. 'I know how much the farm means to you

— and your family. Like Swallow House, it's been handed down from previous generations. Hal, I have to tell you I can't have children. I can't give you an heir. I caught Rubella when I was thirteen and because of a few problems last year, I had tests done. One of the conclusions was that I was infertile.' She hardly dared look at him.

'Jenny, my darling Jenny, I'm so sorry.'

'Yes.' She looked at the ground. 'I should have told you before and of course, I understand you won't want our relationship to go any further.'

The next instant she felt his arms around her drawing her to him. Without a word, he kissed her tenderly. 'You're what I want.' His eyes looked into hers, full of unconditional love. 'Will you marry me, Jenny?'

Dizzy with relief, Jennifer clung to him. 'Oh yes, Hal, yes.'

'And we do have our own child, we've got Ellie. I can't see Anthony wanting to take responsibility. We could adopt her, make it legal. Don't forget, she's a blood relation already.'

'Oh Hal, I love you so very much.'

He drew her close and kissed her lingeringly.

Neither noticed but above them a rainbow appeared, arcing over the green fields as the sun shone out.

Ellie scampered up, her little face alight with joy. 'Look, Auntie Jen, look, pretty colours.'

They followed her gaze and Jennifer drew in her breath. 'She's right, Hal.'

He looked up. 'Seems to me like a pretty good omen, wouldn't you say?'

Jennifer nodded, marvelling, her heart full of love for this man and the child and the wonderful prospect of their future together as a family.

Ellie tugged at her, 'See what I've found, Auntie Jen. I think it's a pretty good omen as well.' She nodded firmly. ''S lovely.'

There, nestling in the palm of her hand, was a perfect white feather.

We do hope that you have enjoyed reading this large print book.

Did you know that all of our titles are available for purchase?

We publish a wide range of high quality large print books including:
Romances, Mysteries, Classics
General Fiction
Non Fiction and Westerns

Special interest titles available in large print are:
The Little Oxford Dictionary
Music Book, Song Book
Hymn Book, Service Book

Also available from us courtesy of Oxford University Press:
Young Readers' Dictionary
(large print edition)
Young Readers' Thesaurus
(large print edition)

For further information or a free brochure, please contact us at:

Other titles in the Linford Romance Library:

ENCORE FOR A DREAM

Sheila Lewis

Limelight Theatre, struggling to survive, is temporarily saved when three sisters unexpectedly inherit it. Rosalind, Olivia and Beatrice are captivated by its charm and the loyalty of the company. With no theatrical experience, the girls strive to combine their own careers with working at Limelight — especially with Gil, the dedicated theatre director. However, an ongoing shortage of cash, a disastrous storm and unforseen tragedy threatens everyone's livelihood, while the girls also have to deal with personal emotional turmoil . . .

REAP THE WHIRLWIND

Wendy Kremer

Briana, passionate about environmental protection, is visiting Turtle Island in the Caribbean. When she discovers Phoebe, the elderly owner of the island, is considering selling it to Nick, Briana is concerned that he'd exploit the island. Determined to prevent this, she attempts to establish 'friendly tourism' there instead, although Nick is extremely sceptical. In reality he doesn't want to change a thing — but certainly relishes a fight. But when Phoebe has a heart attack, he blames Briana's new scheme . . .

IN DANGER OF LOVE

Sheila Holroyd

Ellie and the Earl of Arlbury were virtual strangers, but in a war-torn country they were forced to rely on each other to survive. Outside the normal rules of their society they developed a strong bond which drew them ever closer. But then it looked as if their luck had finally run out, the dangers that had pursued them from the start seemed to have triumphed, and they were threatened by a final, tragic parting . . .

LOVE IN THE MIST

Rosemary A. Smith

1883. Charlotte Trent has secured a post as companion to Lina, seventeen-year-old daughter of the handsome Richard Roseby, at Middlepark in Devon, and has promptly fallen in love with her employer. But not everything is quite as it seems at Middlepark . . . When Charlotte finds a bundle of old love letters hidden in her room she wonders who is Madeline? And the mysterious Anna? And what are Richard's true feelings towards the lovely, and recently widowed, Verity Hawksworth?

MOVING ON

Valerie Holmes

Hailey had prepared her younger sister, Kate, for a life at university; a brighter future than her own. But then Kate falls in love with an older man, David, suddenly leaving Hailey free. Meanwhile James, a successful, wealthy but unfulfilled PR Manager, finds his plans foiled when an accident causes him to miss his flight . . . and one kind act surprisingly leads to another . . . Both Hailey and James' lives change as they move on and in the process they discover love.

JJ

TROPICAL NIGHTS

Phyllis Humphrey

Tracy Barnes has a few words for real-estate mogul Gregory Thompson. Infuriating. Obstinate. Presumptuous. He's bought the Hawaiian hotel where she works as assistant manager and she could be forced out of her job. If it wasn't for his charm she'd hate him. But Gregory, confident in his ability to win over the guarded Tracey, plans dinner, dancing, and a moonlit walk. Maybe it's Hawaii, but Gregory hasn't felt this good in years . . . or wanted a woman this badly . . .